PEAK
DEMOCRACY

G.D. Leon

G.D. Leon
Greenwich, CT

This story is a work of fiction. Any resemblance to actual events or persons, living or dead, is entirely coincidental. However, this doesn't mean the events could become very real.

Book Layout ©2013 BookDesignTemplates.com

Peak Democracy / G.D. Leon -- 1st ed.
ISBN 978-0-9977637-1-3

For Michaela—
home is wherever you are.

I look forward to a great future for America—a future in which our country will match its military strength with our moral restraints, its wealth with our wisdom, its power with our purpose.

—John F. Kennedy

We shaped this world, not only with our power and inventive talent, but also with our understanding of democracy and our efforts to perfect the system.

—Jude Dennings

Liberation

Rumbling sounds from driving on coarse streets entered through the walls, but there was no window in the passenger cabin of the armored personnel carrier that would have allowed for orientation. It seemed it had been built specifically for radioactive contamination.

Prison guards in hazmat suits sat silently across from them—the same as on the way in—but this time Jenny and Eduard were not handcuffed and they had real clothes on instead of the orange jumpsuits. Still, it was all mixed up. The guards had given them different clothes than those they had worn when they were arrested; these were too big for Jenny and too small for Eduard. The IDs they had been given back were in the names of Donna Quiroz and Sebastian Best. One of the guards in the prison had frowned for a second when he checked the photos on the IDs, but then he shrugged and turned around.

What does that all mean? thought Eduard.

He turned to Jenny. She had a blank stare as if she could see through the wall, and tears were welling up at the bottoms of her eyes. It looked as if they were sitting on her high cheekbones, just waiting to gush down.

I've never met my parents—I can only imagine how hard it is to lose one parent and not know how the other is doing. Eduard tried to put his arms around her.

"No contact," said one of the guards in an electronic voice.

Eduard stopped in the middle of the movement and looked at the guard, but he could only see his own face mirrored in the visor of the helmet. Eduard had always been tall and slender, but after the previous days in the prison he felt weak and lanky. His shaved head made him look sick.

"Where are you taking us?"

The guard didn't react to his question.

He might as well have fallen asleep, thought Eduard.

"Flagstaff. Outside the contaminated area."

Then he was silent again and Eduard didn't dare to ask another question. The monotone sound of the APC and the sleep deprivation from the last days took their toll and he fell asleep. He woke up again when the vehicle stopped, but he didn't have much time to think. The hatch in the back opened and two armed guards jumped out. The bright light from outside glared at him. Eduard wasn't able to recognize anything outside.

"Up," ordered one of the remaining guards in the vehicle.

CHAPTER ONE

Perfect System

August — July 15, 2041 — 4 Years to Day 0 (Burlington, VT)

" What do you mean, I shouldn't have cancelled my platinum service?" August Remules slammed the door of his car. He was furious, at least by his standards. It was seven o'clock in the morning, already 87 Fahrenheit outside and it felt hotter with every word. He strode down the driveway and turned into the street. It was a dead end running into Lake Champlain at the end.

"I understand that gold doesn't include instant support, but when I switched last year, you guys promised me a four-hour turnaround..." The neck microphone hurt when he shouted, but he couldn't take it off as the Comm-Dongle had no microphone anymore.

Comm-Dongle: that was the short name for the mobile e-communicator sold by The Holding; it was a two-by-one-inch thing that had squeezed smartphones out of the market fifteen years ago.

"I want to talk to your supervisor. He's an actual human being, not another AI, right? ... Ok, I'll hold." August turned into the main street and passed numerous, almost interchangeable houses with solar cells woven into the curtains, the tax-deductible tree in the front yard—stone gardens, interrupted from time to time by an artificial lawn.

He crossed the street without looking. A honk tore him out of his call, back into reality.

A rusty Chevy stopped next to August and a man with a grin on his face shouted out through the open window, "You better watch where you walk! This isn't a pedestrian zone and not all drivers are as nice as I am."

"Niklas!" August forgot he was angry for a moment and grinned. "What's that? Didn't they ban gas-fuelled cars in Vermont?"

"They did, but this is an old-timer which puts it under federal laws. Let's say, it's complicated." Niklas smirked and brushed his hand through his black hair. With his bronze skin and that hair color, he looked more like he was from Latin America or the Mediterranean than from Sweden. He was ten years younger than August. They had met years ago having coffee at the Lakeshore and got chatting, casually at first, but over time they became best friends.

"Anyway, I only got it because it has no traceable electronics. I know you like to walk to work, but you want a ride?"

August shook his head with a smile. He didn't know anybody else who was so frantic about not being traceable. "Sure, why not? Although my phone will make you traceable."

"It's only for a short ride."

August smiled and got into the car. He appreciated the cool air from the air conditioning. The call seamlessly switched to the car speaker.

"It has electronics?" asked August surprised.

Niklas smirked. "No traceable electronics. I put them in myself—"

"Thank you for holding, are you still there?" The operator sounded tinny through the car's speakers.

"Yes, I'm still here." August glanced out the passenger window. The houses turned from suburban to small town as they drove through Burlington's old main street.

Another, less tinny voice came on. "Thank you for waiting. My name is Dave. First let me apologize for your inconvenience. I'll have somebody fix it today."

"Not today—now! My kid has to go to school and the school bus doesn't stop if you don't fix it."

"I understand, but we are still within the eight-hour window."

"Four. I had four hours in my contract." August looked at Niklas and pulled a face. Niklas raised his eyebrows.

"That was in the old scheme. One month ago we sent out an announcement—"

The overly calm demeanor of the supervisor made August even more frantic. "But I never agreed to this change of service... Do you actually understand what this means to me? My coffee machine wasn't working and I had to manually bypass the shower because they both thought I was still asleep. I had to hot-wire the door for the same reason and now I have to walk to the office because the door lock didn't send the release command so the car security system thinks I'm still at home. And all that because your e-alarm has broken. Why don't you build in failsafes?"

The supervisor used August's pause to jump in. "I understand, Mr. Remules, but—"

August frowned at the way the supervisor pronounced his name in perfect French. "Wait a moment, you're another AI. I asked for an actual human being, and don't tell me there are none around. Your CEO will get a complaint as soon as I'm in the office." August hung up without awaiting an answer and stretched his neck.

Niklas grinned. "You are aware that an AI isn't programmed to be afraid of its manager? But I could delete its personality if it'll make you feel better. That's like killing it—"

"That *would* make me feel better." August took two deep breaths though his nose. "No, don't do that, I was just kidding."

Niklas chuckled without looking at him. "You know me well."

Right outside the old town center, they reached a traffic jam. August looked ahead to see what was up, but he couldn't see anything. The sound of drums and whistles wafted into the car when he opened the window, accompanied by heat.

"Riots again?" asked Niklas.

"It seems so..."

August startled when a shadow rushed by the car window and threw something in: a flyer. 'Wake up! You live in a fake democracy. Join the Resistance,' it said. A cop followed the man who had thrown the flyer, but he gave up after two yards and came back to the car.

"Criminals," he said to August and shook his head. "You can give me that crap—maybe they left fingerprints."

"What's going on there?" August gave him the flyer.

The cop shrugged. "Stupid farmers protesting. Seems some lost their jobs to self-driving tractors." He grunted and walked away again.

Niklas turned to August. "You know how useless it is to call that service line? These bots get a better psychological education than many psychologists. I programmed one myself and added sentences that would annoy people, just for the fun of it." Niklas smirked. "Their only job is to deflect you. But why did you cancel the platinum service anyways?"

"You've got it easy; you can program your AIs and automation yourself. Normal people like me have to rely on services, and gold service is just not good enough. I have global responsibilities and need to be on call twenty-four hours. Eight hours without AI could cost me my job."

The line moved a little.

August squinted through the window. "Most of my money goes to debt repayment: mortgage, student loans, you name it. The Holding requires me to have all loans with them. That way they can keep two-thirds of my salary themselves; it goes directly out of my paycheck. After that it's either the AI services or college savings for Jenny, and healthcare. Freaking healthcare—50% increase just because I was born abroad. Do you get this?" August tapped his fist against his forehead. "They can't evaluate the healthcare from where I was born. I bear a healthcare risk. Compared to the US, the healthcare system in Switzerland is Zero World, not First World."

"I get it, but you must be doing something wrong. I don't have that problem. They seem to be able to evaluate Sweden correctly."

"I don't know. It just seemed better to cancel the platinum service than to fall behind on healthcare. Frustrating, I never wanted to be at that point. I thought I had a career." August sighed. "I guess I have to do better. Maybe being Chief Information Officer of The Holding would get me somewhere." August shook his head, staring into space. He noticed that Niklas wanted to say something comforting, but he was happy he didn't. Sometimes things don't need to be said between friends. August tried to move his annoyance away; starting a work day as aggravated as he was would only end in disaster.

The streets had been cleared of protesters in the meantime and they were moving again. August could already see The Holding's logo on the multiplex building, an overly large logo on a clunky brick. These buildings had popped up all over the country in the twenties of the new century. They offered comprehensive infrastructure-related services, from networking and security to food courts and fitness areas.

These multiplex buildings are an ingenious invention. I should have had the idea.

The cost of living in the hot city centers had become far too expensive for most people and the commute to less expensive areas too long to be absorbable. Companies started to allow people to work from home, but this created an even bigger problem. August chuckled to himself. He remembered too well the distractions when his daughter was a toddler; "Daddy" here, "Daddy" there. He had even heard of real excesses, like people privately offshoring their tasks or creating apps to appear online. He had used a more brick-and-mortar trick: place the mouse on an analog watch and the constant movements of the second hand would do the rest.

"I was just thinking how these multiplex buildings started," said August, trying to move Niklas' thoughts away as well.

"Well, to be honest, when the first ones popped up in South Carolina and Tennessee, I thought they'd disappear again soon. I was working for Bank of America back then and they wanted our entire department to move down there, accompanied by a 30% pay cut, but they had no space. They offered for me to work up here—of course with the same pay cut."

August frowned and shook his head. "But back then this was an ordinary office building, not a multiplex. Only the new owners transformed it."

"Guess who the new owners were? Right: The Holding."

"They sold the building to themselves? Hmm. Anyway, if you think about it now, it was a natural development—"

"*FAN!*" Niklas shouted to the driver who had just cut him off. As he slammed on the brakes, the seatbelt cut into August's shoulder.

"It probably wasn't even his fault. The auto-drive system didn't see you." August looked at the car in front of them. Through the rear window he could see the guy reading the newspaper.

Niklas raised one eyebrow. "Very comforting."

"You should switch on your transponder. It's mandatory for these old cars."

"And be traceable? No way." Niklas shook his head without taking his eyes off the street. He turned into the parking lot of the multiplex building; there were only uncovered spaces left. "Perfect. This car will be an oven by the evening." He shrugged.

"Lucky me, I don't have to drive back with you," said August when they got out.

Niklas tilted his head with a questioning look.

"I'm giving a guest speech at the university."

"Sounds fun." Niklas waved and walked towards the side entrance.

August knew that Niklas worked in a highly secured area with no connection to the rest of the building, but that entrance looked more like an unloading dock for trucks. August shrugged. *Maybe hiding in plain sight is the best tactic,* he thought while he was walking to the main entrance.

Inside the building August was reminded again of the very unpleasant start to the day. He had not been able to check out at home, which caused the security gate to deny him access. The identification desk was around the corner, but he wasn't the only one with this problem—it seemed the service outage had not been an isolated event. August sighed as he saw the long line of managers in front of the desk.

This will take me at least a half an hour, he sighed. Although the identification was based on a three-second iris scan, 100 times three seconds, plus twelve seconds per person for moving forward, equals twenty-five minutes—simple math.

Until he was cleared, he wouldn't be able to move his meetings via his Comm-Dongle; he couldn't even get his messages on his VR goggles. *Somehow the linking of everything together made the whole thing fragile.* He wondered where they would stop.

"My daughter got a loan for her wedding—can you imagine?" said one of the managers in front of him to another. "How crazy is that?"

He was about August's age, a little greyer maybe. He sounded older and his suspenders made him look as if he came from another century. August didn't know him, but he had worked with the other guy on a project; August tried to remember which one, but who recalls every project they have worked on? He knew he worked for The Holding's legal department.

"Getting a loan is even easier than buying a gun," said Legal Department Guy, "but beware of the consequences. I've seen this too many times. If there's the slightest risk of defaulting, her cost of living will go through the roof: the interest on her loans, her healthcare cost, even her rent. Don't ask me how they calculate the risk—for that you need an IT guy with a doctorate in math." He was unstoppable.

The one with the suspenders already regretted having started the conversation. "And guess what?" he was finally able to throw in. "I'll be the one picking up the tab when something goes wrong—all for the family."

The other guy ignored his words. "Eventually she'll also lose her job because she's a 'higher risk for fraud and irregularities to a company'. The Supreme Court ruled on this years ago."

"Isn't that crazy? The future of the nation is defined by the mortality of judges. That's the same as if the president were elected by throwing a dice."

Legal Department Guy shrugged. "There was an outcry back then and now it's business as usual. I've seen many go down simply because they were one day late with an invoice or, even worse, when the loan company made a mistake. As soon as the avalanche is moving, you don't stand a chance." He raised his arms to the side and shrugged again. "The trailer park cities in the Midwest are full of managers who landed in that trap, and the graveyards are full of those who acted upon it. But this is the system. We are just too willing to run up debt—an expensive MBA here, a 200-person wedding there, and everybody needs the most sophisticated AI on top. It's simple: it's their own fault."

Suspender Guy had stopped listening. His eyes were wandering around the hall.

He's right. I have to take care that the data I'm protecting is not abused, even within The Holding, August thought. *I don't want to be the cause of somebody's misery, and the data of the Valkyrie Microfinance Company can easily be abused. Information about loans at risk leads to a veritable disaster for the borrower.*

"Stop him!" The commotion brought August back into reality. A man who had been first in the line was running zigzag through the hall, followed by a handful of security officers. "Stop him!" one of them shouted again. Too many foxes are the rabbit's defeat; one of the guards took him down with a Taser.

While the security brought the unconscious man to a side door, a murmur went through the line. August caught things like "an imposter" and "Resistance tried to infiltrate".

The guy looked familiar, but August couldn't place who he was.

Without further trying, August just stood and watched; the thrill deadens after having seen it a few times. Just a dull angst remains. *One defaulted loan and that could be you.*

#

When August finally got into the building, more bad news was waiting for him. The occupancy panel showed free offices only on the top floor. *Damn, that's the only thing I hate about these multiplex buildings. It wouldn't have to be a corner office—just every day the same, my office.* The top-floor offices could get as hot as 95 Fahrenheit. August selected a corner office with views onto

Lake Champlain. The green light above the door turned red when he unlocked the room with his iris scan. He wasn't that worried about the temperature; right now it was still bearable, and he would be out in the afternoon. He was more worried about what else would not work due to the incident that morning, but everything was working when he put his Comm-Dongle in the docking station: the e-pad and the large screen came up with his communication module and the documents where he had left them before the weekend. At least the visit to the identification desk had set back the office configurations.

Every office was equipped with a docking station to access your virtual machine, a large screen on the wall, an e-pad and, August's favorite gadgets, a meeting booth for virtual meetings and a glove to swoosh around files and programs between all devices. But what he loved most was the AI voice module. August had named her Alex.

"Alex."

"Good morning, Mr. Remules. What can I do for you?" said a dark female voice with a Russian accent. Niklas had helped him to program that non-standard nuance. "The only tricky part to adapt," he had said, "was removing the perfect French accent when Alex says 'Remules'."

"Daily planning routine." August suppressed the urge to call the manager of the AI from that morning. He sighed. *Niklas is right; that would be useless.*

"Sure. Weekly outlook importan—"

"Skip."

The AI's voice seemed impervious to his annoyed tone. "News—"

"Meetings and overdue tasks first." *I need to change that routine,* thought August.

"Today. Daily planning, 7.30AM, missed. Update call with team, 7.45AM, missed. Three messages."

"Move update call with team to tomorrow. Find a slot."

"Invitation sent. Automated data transfer to SURE, 10AM. Guest speech, 1PM at the University of Vermont. Tasks: call *New York Times* journalist re: interview."

August pulled a face. He had procrastinated over this task for a week. He was only allowed to give this interview because the *Times* was part of The Holding. These interviews were just boring and took time away from the day: pre-arranged answers to pre-arranged questions.

"News: the border protection legislation passed the EU parliament..."

August's thoughts faded away as he marvelled at the view. The building was located at the end of Queneska Peninsula, and from today's office he could see across Lake Champlain, far into the Adirondacks. The water was sparkling in the sun, and on the horizon he could make out a flock of Canada geese travelling south. He enjoyed the view for a moment; tomorrow he might be able to get an office on a lower level.

"...polls for the upcoming elections show a vast majority for the European People's Party. no more news. Three messages. Play the messages now?" Alex's voice interrupted his thoughts.

"Play messages," August said towards the desk.

"Team meeting, message one: 'August, you owe me. It's the third time now. You top the list of missed meetings.'"

August had to smile. Lorenzo was the joker of the team, but what a bright mind. He was living down in Key West.

"Team meeting, message two: 'Ey, August, sorry to bring it up again, but I need you to sign off my vacation...'"

August interrupted the AI's flow. "New task: sign off Daniel's vacation, priority high, due today."

"Task logged. New message, received today, 7.45AM, from Jude Dennings, priority high: 'Hi August, call me. We have to align our positions. We already agreed on the request, so no surprises at ten o'clock, right?' No more messages."

Align our positions? August thought with a little grim grin on his face. *That means adopt his view.*

"Shade windows."

The crystals in the windows turned it to a transparent charcoal. Keeping the sunlight out was the best tactic to avoid a sauna in the afternoon, and at the same time the crystals served as a solar panel.

August scratched his chin. *It's astonishing what progress can be achieved if we have to. And all because of the nuclear meltdown of Palos Verde.* After the terrorist attack it had taken less than five years to switch off all but three nuclear power plants. It had been the hour of solar cells and batteries.

He grabbed the e-pad and swooshed the files for the meeting onto the screen while he walked over to the couch. *This deal is a veritable career-killer,* he thought when he went through his notes again. *I agree and something goes wrong, they hang me. If I don't agree, Dennings will make sure I get hanged right away.* The insurance company SURE had requested access to the company's database. SURE was one of the reckless companies within The

Holding; they had found out that over 45% of their claims came from people whose loans defaulted less than one year later. Some bright guy had the idea to procrastinate on paying out these claims until the defaulting happened, but for that they would need the predictive data models from August's data scientists and the underlying data of Valkyrie. Technically that would not be a problem—

A signal indicating an incoming call interrupted him. August narrowed his eyes when he saw the caller's identity: Donna, the group's Chief Information Officer.

"Answer, voice only."

He liked her, but her stubbornness had gotten her into trouble before. *You'd better stay out of her way when she gets started, even though most of the time she's right.*

"August, I assume you got a call from Dennings as well?" Donna had never been a big fan of small talk on the phone, but today she seemed particularly gruff. She continued without waiting for his answer. "I can offer some free advice: don't sign that contract."

"What's your concern?"

"It would violate the anti-trust regulations. The Department of Justice only allowed The Holding to form if we kept the business in silos with Chinese walls between them. You know exactly what I'm talking about."

"Yeah, but if Legal and Risk agree, who am I to deny it?" August shook his head.

"I've got some legal advice of my own. The Department of Justice will see this data sharing as violation of anti-trust law. If you sign, they will use you as a scapegoat."

"I see, let me think about it."

"I will not sign. They'll need to replace me if they want the group CIO's signature." She paused for a second. "And don't trust Dennings. I've seen too many people go and they never saw it coming. He plays dirty games."

"Don't worry. I'll be cautious. But thanks for the warning."

A beep-bop sound indicated that she had already closed the communication. *No, she doesn't trust Dennings at all—and neither do I.* Dennings was the shooting star of The Holding, a guy in his mid-thirties with a career like a rocket. But Jude Dennings was also known for always having an agenda. August sure didn't want to be one of his victims.

"New message. Sign-off matrix from Pradeep Singh," said Alex with her dark female voice.

August looked up at the screen on the wall and furrowed his brows. Sign-off matrix from his boss? He hadn't missed a sign-off last week, had he?

Alex's voice interrupted him again before he could check his open action list. "Meeting cancel request: automated data transfer to SURE, today, 10AM."

Something's rotten in the state of Denmark. He switched to the communication module on the e-pad. *They wanted this so badly and now they cancel the meeting?* He took a moment, and then he got up and swooshed the two items next to each other on the screen. He stood in front of them as if he couldn't believe it. The meeting had been cancelled and instead he had received the simple sign-off page for the request. Everybody else had already signed off, including Jude, August's boss, the two company CEOs and the heads of Risk and Legal. August shook his head and sighed. He looked back at the screen. Donna was missing; she was not even required to sign. He frowned. The deadline for him to sign was today at noon.

Then he realized it—the real plot, the Machiavellian move. Every signature had a date in the future—only by eight days, but nonetheless in the future. August held his breath for a second. He opened his mouth to say a command, but no sound came out. He jumped to his e-pad and opened the communicator. *This is Dennings' doing.* Right before calling him, August stopped. He walked over to the blackened window, turned around and then went to the water dispenser. *If this is fraudulent, I don't want to be part of this.* It wouldn't need a conviction; just substantiated allegations alone would trigger a default on August's loans. His hands were shaking as he filled a cup, and he spilled some as he drank it in one go. Afterwards he felt able to speak again without the urge to vomit, but he needed somebody to spill out his head to.

"Call Donna." August's voice was still shaking. Maybe she knew something; at least she was in the headquarters in Fairview.

"Call failed. User inactive," said Alex.

August jerked his head back and took deep breath. *They didn't fire her for not signing, did they?* With all he had seen so far in the office, this was messed up on a whole other level.

"Text Niklas, 'Hey buddy, you have time for a quick coffee?'"

"Text sent."

August stood in the middle of the room as if it was a funnel and he didn't know yet which direction to take to get out. Finally, what felt like an eternity later, Alex said, "New text: 'Sure, buddy. Usual spot.'"

He grabbed the Comm-Dongle and was already out the door before Alex finished the message. The door locked automatically behind him.

#

Niklas

Niklas knew where to go. Since they had become close friends, it had happened almost every other day that one or the other needed to vent. August was already waiting on the boardwalk outside the Lakeshore with his venti coffee and a quadruple espresso.

"Hey mate, what's up? You look even worse than this morning." He gave August a clap on his shoulder. "Whatever it is, remember: be fit and survive."

August forced a smile and Niklas had the impression that a couple of jokes wouldn't be enough this time. August took a deep breath and told Niklas about the request, Donna's phone call and Jude Dennings' maneuver. Niklas looked out on the lake while August was talking. *Poor August. I'm so glad I'm not part of senior management.* In the corner of his eyes he noticed that August had almost crushed his cup with his hand. Niklas wondered why he didn't feel the pressure like August did. It could be his level in The Holding's hierarchy—Niklas was a database specialist on the bottom of the food chain—but it could also be the all or nothing of it. Once you default, you're done.

He waited patiently, blowing out air through his nose from time to time. When he got the feeling August had finished, he asked, still looking out on the lake, "And who do you blame?"

August didn't answer.

Niklas snorted. "Where have you been? This is reality. What do you think, my friend? How many times a day do I have to do something a) mindless, b) meaningless, c) just because a *manager* wants to have it or d) to cover up somebody else's unethical plots?" He stopped and bit his lip. *That was a little too harsh.* "I refused two or three times. You wanna guess what happened?"

Niklas turned to August, who was looking down at the wrecked coffee cup in his hands. He felt a little pity for his miserable-looking friend, but he had to hear this.

"Somebody else did it, got promoted and got a salary increase. I know you're different, but I got the check for my good conscience. Look at me: I live outside town in an old industrial complex, I don't wear expensive clothes and all my money goes into my computers. Wake up, August. Don't you think your Jude Dennings already got the data via another channel? He's made sure the whole deal pays. I bet those corporate big data scientists have already done the analysis and now they need a regular data feed. You surprise me."

August looked up with eyes wide open.

"You're so strategic and cautious in your thinking and then you throw everything overboard in a heartbeat, simply based on a gut feeling or a mood." Then the pity kicked in. "See, your approval has nothing to do with the real world, it's not worth the electricity it uses. It's the same as if you stole something in your friend's house and asked after the fact if you could borrow it. And like Jude Dennings, you just never return it," he added smiling. "Sign it and forget about it."

"Maybe you're right." August nodded.

Niklas stood up. "Of course I am. The sign-off date in the future is odd, though." He shrugged.

August got up as well. It seemed he had calmed down a little.

He's too nice. Sometimes I wonder which of us is older and wiser, Niklas thought.

"By the way, did you hear about the intruder this morning?" Niklas tried to guide August's thoughts in a different direction.

August nodded. "I saw it, poor guy."

"And did you recognize him?"

"No, should I have?" August held the door for Niklas when they entered the building.

"It was the former CEO of The Holding's logistics company. You remember? The one they fired a month ago? He had all his loans with The Holding and lost everything: house, car, boat, wife. Apparently he was caught speaking up against how the system treats people who defaults on their loans. There were also posts he made on social media. That triggered a risk flag in the system, which made his loans default. Isn't that ironic? He came back because he wanted to get proof of something, at least that's what people are saying on the floor."

"Poor guy," said August again, but Niklas wasn't sure if he had actually listened.

#

They separated in front of the high-security entrance and Niklas went down to his office in the basement. He didn't have to fight for an office like the others, and he never had an issue with the temperature down there. As a database specialist he sat right in the center of the north-east data hub of The Holding. Together with the technicians, there were only seven people with direct access to the server rooms.

Ten floors beneath ground level the elevator door opened. The server room looked like something from a bad science-fiction movie. It was two stories high and divided by a glass wall into a large server part and a tiny office area. The floor and the walls were tiled in white. Seven desks stood in the office area, each equipped with virtual-reality glasses and gloves for the developers. Only the supervisor's desk had an actual screen from where he could switch from one set of VR glasses to another. Niklas chuckled. This moron could watch him the entire time without having a clue what he was actually doing.

"Welcome back to our sacred halls. How is the temperature outside?" David, one of the IT technicians, had taken off his VR glasses and was eating his breakfast. The chair he was sitting in appeared far too small for his hips.

"Reaching 87, I guess." Niklas walked towards his desk.

"Puh, happy to be down here during the day. I hate to sweat."

You sweat like a pig. Niklas tried not to inhale while he passed him.

"You met your manager friend, right? Did he know anything about when they will move us?" David licked his fingers.

"I don't talk about projects with him and he wouldn't even know. This project is top secret. I hope *you* don't talk about Project OneHub outside."

David put his VR glasses back on and all Niklas got was a grunt as an answer. He shrugged and went back to work, only to be interrupted minutes later by Michal, the project leader of the OneHub project. Niklas' hackles rose when he saw the name pop up on his screen. *Asshole* flashed through his mind and he resisted the urge to decline the call.

He picked up and Michal's voice yelled into his ear. "Soderberg, you're not supposed to leave the secured area during the day. We didn't install a pantry and a kitchen down there for nothing. I need your status on the safeguard software for the program workshop."

It's Soderstrom, you idiot. Niklas tried to stay calm and took a breath before answering. "I sent it yesterday night to the project management office, at 11PM my time. You were copied in on it. Let me check. Yeah, here it is, Michal Kolamtov, but you have to look in the secured mailbox."

The voice grunted. "I don't read e-mails from people of a lower rank than director. Just brief me on the sub-streams. Anti-malware/anti-spyware stream?" Michal's voice had something that grated on Niklas like nails on a chalkboard.

"Green, code delivered and tested. User acceptance test pending." Niklas tried to give the updates in as monotone a voice as possible.

"Database integrity module?" scratched Michal's voice.

Niklas made a game out of these calls: how long does it take until Michal gets angry? "There are difficulties—"

"How many times have I told you how I want this? First the red-amber-green status," Michal almost shrieked.

Niklas sighed but chuckled. "Amber, they delivered the—"

"No amber, you have to set it back to green."

"But we have to send the code back to the developers. There are some issues they have to fix."

"You can fix it right? Otherwise why do we need an expensive database specialist in the US, when we could have two offshore?"

"You need to have coding and data encryption capabilities to do so—that's why you would need three people offshore to replace me. And to answer your question: yes, I could fix it myself, however it would be against policy if I did."

"Listen, Soderberg, delaying the project helps neither you nor the project. This is a career-killer. Fix it. If you need master key access rights to the back end, just order them and I will approve. Next, audit module?"

"Also amber, do you want me to fix this too?" Niklas sighed.

"You are a quick learner, I like that. I assume your coworker is up to date on the code, in case they want the program to off-shore more people?"

"Aye, sir—"

Michal hung up before Niklas finished talking. He threw his headset on the desk. *What a Monday morning,* he thought. *What did I tell August this morning? Well, the universe has a dark sense of humor.* He frowned for a moment and slowly shook his head. *Michal hasn't the faintest idea what I could do with those access rights.* For a moment Niklas wasn't sure if it was that thought or the smell of David's breakfast getting into his nose that made him nauseous.

#

August

Back in the office, August could already feel that it would become a greenhouse later in the afternoon. He was happy he would get out for the speech at the university. Every other term, the university invited professionals from all over the country to give guest speeches during their education initiative days. August participated regularly, mostly because it was conveniently close and it counted for the mandatory volunteering hours in the office.

August checked the time. *Damn, noon. No time for lunch today. Again.* He picked the e-pad up and his finger wavered for a moment above the screen as he pulled a face, before he swooshed the data transfer request back on the screen. It was as if the future dates were mocking him. A little devil on his shoulder came up with an idea he liked.

"Create support ticket."

"Please describe the issue," answered Alex promptly.

"Document #CT2025-#07439662 has an issue with the time stamp/time zone synchronization. Certain modifications including signature appear in the future."

"Please add screenshot."

"Not possible, classification of the document is set to highly confidential. I will keep a copy in my files for evidence purposes."

"Priority?"

"High."

"Ticket #07072025-15356 is open and pending allocation."

"Create certified virtual print of the ticket and store it in my personal zone."

"Saved."

August smirked and clapped himself on the shoulders in his mind. *If anything is fishy with that request, I'll be able to pull that ticket. They'll have to get up earlier to get ahead of me.* Satisfied, he turned back to the contract and looked at it for a moment. He knew they would be sitting on tenterhooks, waiting for him to sign. "So let's let them wait," he said to himself and looked at his task list. 'Call *New York Times* journalist re: interview' was still listed for today.

"Call Roberta what's-her-face at the *New York Times*."

"There is nobody with that name at the *New York Times*. However, there is a Henry Robert, a Roberta Bloomington and a Roberta Jones."

"Roberta Bloomington."

A moment later Roberta's husky voice came on. "Hi, this is Roberta. Well, not actually, but virtually. Leave a message and I'll call you back. I promise."

She seemed to be one of the rare people still using a voicemail instead of a personal AI. Well, he too could have used Alex to set up the meeting, but he wanted to hear the voice to have a feeling for the person.

"Hi, Roberta, this is August from Valkyrie Microfinance. I understand you want to meet me for an interview. Somehow my AI can't connect with yours. Next Monday, 10AM would work for me. Let me know."

"Meeting alert," came Alex's voice. "Education initiative, 1PM this afternoon at the university. As you are going by foot, I suggest you leave in twenty minutes."

August turned back to the screen. He still had to sign the request. With his virtual glove, he signed it in the air and the signature appeared on the screen. The arrow was already hovering above the accept button, but something was strange. August blinked in disbelief. He had to step closer to make he saw right, but he was not mistaken. The time stamp that appeared next to his signature was next Tuesday—the same day as the other signatures.

August shook his head. *All that fuss about nothing. Apparently, the future time stamp was only an IT glitch.* He took a deep breath, packed his messenger bag and left. The light outside the office went back to green.

#

It took him half the time the system had calculated, but he didn't mind being early. He loved to stroll around the campus and have lunch in the food court. He always felt at home at universities, be it at the campus here in Burlington or at his Alma Mater in Stanford. While walking over the campus, he got a text message that the issues at home were fixed.

Exactly eight hours. It's as if they waited for the last moment of the service-level agreement. Idiots.

It was already busy at the Ben & Jerry's building when he arrived, and he fought his way through the crowd until he found the right classroom. This year the event was popular, and he found the room already packed with students.

He looked around and a multitude of colored eyes looked back. This year, adaptive colored contact lenses were in. They changed color depending on the mood of the person wearing them. Green meant harmony and equilibrium, red was joy, and yellow was anger or hate. Interestingly, violet meant love and pink meant horny. Right now, most of the eyes were just blue, brown or green, but some were red and August thought he had seen one pink. He chuckled. *Good job we were able to convince Jenny to suppress pink.*

"Welcome to this guest lecture. My name is August Remules; I'm Chief Data Officer at the Valkyrie Microfinance Company. Like many other companies, we are owned by The Holding."

A student with oversized glasses in the first row held his hand up. August called on him and added that everybody could interrupt with questions.

"You are Chief Data Officer of one of The Holding's companies."

August nodded.

"Does that mean every company has your role, and if yes, isn't that inefficient?" The student leaned back as if he had asked a very important question.

August smirked. "The Holding was founded with excess cash from one the largest hedge funds. As they continued to buy, the Department of Justice obliged The Holding to keep each company separate. Any other questions?"

August paused and looked around.

"Ok, then let me start by telling you a little more about myself. My family emigrated from Switzerland when I was nine years old and settled here in Burlington. My dad was a watchmaker back in his home town. Here he opened a watch store, and as a little side business he repaired them in his shop. He didn't make big money, but he was able to help get me a decent education. Later, after Stanford, I got hired by eCove."

A murmur went through the room.

"Yes, you heard right. I was there from when they moved out of the garage through to when they were bought by Valkyrie. Back then Valkyrie was still an online retail store."

"Sir?" interrupted one of the students and half-heartedly raised his hand.

"Call me August, please."

The student blushed. "How did you finance Stanford?"

"I had a little scholarship and I worked on the side, but mostly through an insane student loan. But honestly, you're better off here. Solid education at a reasonable price. You should have a chance to pay back your student loans before your kids go to college."

Another murmur went through the students, but this time it sounded more like a grumble.

A girl in the back raised her hand. She was the one with the pink eye color. "I don't understand that system. It forces you into debt and kicks you out at the first mistake. Wouldn't it make more sense to keep the borrower on and let him pay for as long as he can rather than just defaulting immediately?"

"First, it's a natural thing that you have financial problems when you're young and investment problems later, but nobody forces you into debt. It's always your own decision to buy that new car or go on that vacation. And second, the system has to be hard otherwise people would take advantage of it." *And, most importantly, they can always get their money back from either loan insurance or the Global Microfinance Fund.*

"But that's not a discussion for here," added August and flipped his eyes around the room. No more questions. He took a deep breath.

CHAPTER TWO

Achilles' Heel

August – July 21 – 4 Yeats to Day 0 (Burlington, VT)

Sunday evening, August and Jenny were sitting on the porch, contemplating the front lawn. The Remules still had a real lawn in their garden, unlike the other houses with their stone gardens or fake lawns. The buzzing of the electromagnetic fly screen around the porch was the only sound.

"There!" squeaked Jenny and pointed to a glimpse of light. Her blonde hair fluttered and fell back into her face. She brushed it out the way. Jenny had the same sporty shape her mother had had when they married, and the same high cheekbones which seemed even higher when she beamed.

August just saw the light of the firefly before it disappeared again. "There's another one."

"I so love fireflies. Remember that summer when the lawn was full?" Jenny gazed out on the lawn, hoping to catch another one, but it seemed they never appeared in the same spot twice.

"I do." He smiled. *It was past midnight before Olivia and I could get you to bed.* "It's a pity your friend at school can't enjoy something like this. What was her name? Rosie?"

Jenny pouted. "Rosetta. Don't get me started on her. She wears white gloves now, as if we were filthy. If you touch one of her things, they call you to the principal's office."

"That's not her fault." August pressed his lips together. "She's allergic to other people's sebum. We have somebody in the office who has the same. You should be glad you're healthy."

"I'm sorry. I didn't mean..."

August took her into his arms. He paused for a moment to put the words right. "You are a wonderful person."

"Please, Daddy, don't ruin it with one of those 'the world is bad' speeches."

"No, the world is neither good nor bad. It's the people that are good or bad."

"I know that. I really do, but I'm not willing to accept it. It must be possible to make this world a better place."

"You are a truly good person. But that doesn't prevent you from making bad decisions." Last week's sign-off came to August's mind again. *I just did exactly that.* A tingling feeling spread in his stomach. "There's always somebody who will want you to do something that's not OK, offering a quick way out of all your hardship. I see people being caught every week and, once caught, they're practically unemployable."

Jenny leaned back, crossed her arms in front of her chest and narrowed her eyebrows. The magic of the fireflies seemed far away.

"I just want you to think twice before you act. Everything you do is logged and available for internal investigation and even prosecution in case of an offense." August's stomach crumbled. *I need to ask Niklas if he can check on that ticket.*

"I knew you would ruin it. You and mom always say that you trust me, just to take it back again later. You told me that a thousand times."

"That's not true, I simply want..." August broke off. The vibrant beginning had died off in a vacuum of missing arguments and topics. He had killed the moment. But Jenny wasn't walking away like she had done before; she sat there and looked into the night. It was almost as if August could read her thoughts, something along the lines that next year she would be out and would prove herself to everybody.

She's like me: the brain in constant dispute with the gut.

In that moment August pledged to himself, as he had when he had held her for the first time, that he would protect her from any harm with every means he had—even with his life if he had to.

#

July 22

On his way to the interview with Roberta, August wanted to go through the questions and answers once more, but he dropped the idea. *What a waste of time*, he thought when he walked through the automatic doors at the Lakeshore Plaza mall. He had already delivered the answers to The Holding's PR department. They had forwarded them to the *New York Times*. As if that was not enough control, the *Times* would send the finished article back to the PR department for review. *Whatever*. Going to this interview was like watching beginners golfing—you don't even bother to duck when somebody shouts "Four!"

The New York Times, the Washington Post, FOX Today—they're all the same. What a shame. August uttered a chuckle.

They'd still be independent if the internet hadn't caught them sleeping. When they woke up, they were already in the arms of The Holding and half the staff lighter. Only a few real journalists remained; Roberta was among them. Even though he hated the idea of this interview, he had still checked her out. *You have to know your counterpart.* He entered the coffee shop in the Lakeshore Plaza and looked around. *Ah, there she is.*

She had got hold of one of the tables with the sofas at the window and was enjoying the view of the lake. The coffee shop was not very busy for an ordinary Monday morning; two hikers were talking to some sailing tourists around the tables in the middle of the room, two businessmen were discussing something at the bar and a group of elderly ladies were enjoying an early morning chat at the window. The coffee shop was perfect for the interview; The Holding had financed a privacy function for the tables at the window. White noise prevented people sitting close by from accidentally eavesdropping.

Roberta was still gazing out of the window when August came to the table. The high backrest of the sofas prevented her from noticing him.

"Good morning, Roberta. I'm August."

"Oh, good morning, August. I'm sorry, I was enjoying the view a little too much, I guess." She jumped up and offered her hand with a sassy smile, one that only lifted one corner of her mouth. She had warm, ice-grey eyes that matched her grey hair, which she had bound back into a ponytail.

August forgot to shake her hand and felt stupid when he realized it. "Not your fault. It is breathtaking."

"It must be a gift to work here." His faux pas made her smile even sassier.

August looked down for a second. "It's a gift to live here. Please." He made a gesture to sit. "I assume you received my answers," he said while he switched on the privacy mode. An almost unnoticeable noise swallowed the sound of the coffee shop.

"I did, but I have additional questions."

He hesitated a second and asked slowly, "Are they authorized?"

She smiled again, but more serious this time. "They're not new questions, just clarifications of some answers." She took out her notebook and a small recorder that looked like it came from another century.

August fizzled out a cry. "You're a Teta Teta Teta!" He pointed to the print on the notebook.

She tilted her head and the smile disappeared from her lips, but not without the corners of her mouth tweaking twice.

"Truth Through Truth." August smirked and the longer she took to react, the more sheepish he felt.

She blinked. August had the impression it was the first time she had blinked since they had met two minutes ago.

"I studied at Georgetown and I joined the society because I hated the separation between fraternities and sororities. Truth Through Truth guided my through my entire career," she said finally.

August breathed a silent sigh of relief. "I met my wife in the society and she has guided me since then. I went to Stanford and she went to Berkeley—natural enemies. It's a miracle we found each other. I miss those days. She would be thrilled to meet you."

"I planned to stay for two days. Maybe we can have coffee together."

He closed his mouth for a second before he opened it again. "Why don't you come for dinner tomorrow night? We would be thrilled to have you over."

"Only if you answer my questions." Roberta winked and brought up her sassy smile again. "Do you have access to my data?"

"This is off the record, right?" August peered at the recorder in front of him.

She grabbed the recorder and put it away. "Completely. Triple-T guarantee. No way I'd put something like this into the article—The Holding would use it as an excuse to execute me, professionally speaking."

"Then why ask them?" August frowned.

"You know the tale of the frog and the scorpion?"

August raised his eyebrows, rubbing his chin.

"Well, it goes like this: a scorpion asks a frog to carry him across a river. At first, the frog doesn't want to, afraid of being stung, but the scorpion says that if he did that, they both would drown. The frog agrees, but in the middle of the river, the scorpion stings the frog. Drowning, the frog asks why the scorpion did that. The scorpion replies that it had to, it's in its nature."

August leaned back and smiled, understanding.

"I'm a journalist. It's in my nature to ask questions. Why don't you ask me something first—anything?" When August didn't answer right away she added, "Truth calls for truth—ask away."

August thought for a second. "You've won almost every prize out there, except for the Pulitzer. Why?"

Roberta took a deep breath; August immediately felt sorry for the question, but she answered without losing countenance. "I assume I'm too annoying. In the last decades I've broken uncountable *Times* rules, but I guess I'm too famous to get rid of and too dangerous to decorate. Sometimes I think they would love to send me off to a war zone and award me the Pulitzer when I return in a box. Not that I don't want to win it, but not at the cost of being buried."

"I'm sorry I brought it up."

"No worries. The place at the wall is anyway taken by my grandchild and no way I replace that picture." She smirked and her smirk looked even sassier than her smile. "Now, my question: do you have access to my data?"

"Technically yes," August said, "I do have access, but that's logged."

"Did you check it out before meeting me?"

"For sure not, but I did a little internet research."

"Are there price agreements with the competition?"

"Not that I'm aware of."

"But with the constant interchange of employees between The Holding and The Corp one could assume there is at least a common understanding of a non-aggression pact. Only dinosaurs like me get life with The Holding."

August mumbled something and he wasn't sure himself what he wanted to say.

"Do you share data with The Corp? I mean the *competition*?"

"Not at all." This answer came loud and clear.

Roberta put on a look as if she could pick up a scent. "Really?"

August shook his head, but his thoughts went to what Niklas had told him. "We don't *share* data, but there is always a cost pressure on whatever we do. And with all these compliance obligations, the National IT Security Act bears the biggest burden..."

"Well, you don't share your data centers, right?"

August raised his eyebrows.

It took Roberta a couple of seconds to pick up the thought, but then she continued with an undertone of disbelief August had not heard from her yet. "You share your back-up data center? No way."

"Not exactly. The Holding outsources the maintenance of the data centers to a third-party provider. Coincidentally, The Holding and The Corp use the same provider—just under different brands. You have to understand, even as a Chief Data Officer I wouldn't know if it wasn't for my friend who happens to work for said provider."

"I get the feeling your take on The Holding isn't much better than mine." Roberta blew out air through her nose.

August shook his head. "It's not as bad as it sounds. There are just some angles that could make it difficult from time to time. But every company has bad apples and sometimes it's just me overreacting. It's not always ill will when mistakes happen."

"I can hardly imagine you overreacting." She squinted through the window at something on the lake.

August hesitated a moment and then told her about last week's episode with the signatures and his suspicions that he had been the victim of an intrigue.

He closed with, "It turned out to be an IT glitch. I followed up last Friday, but they haven't found the issue yet. Well, it's not so critical anymore. The dates are as of tomorrow anyway. After that it's a normal contract. Everything all right?" Roberta had turned back to him. "You look puzzled."

"I hate to be right sometimes, but are you sure this has nothing to do with the ruling the Supreme Court expected for today?"

"Which ruling?"

"Miller against *The Poste*."

August tilted his head. "Miller against *The Poste*?"

"It hasn't been big in the news. I only know about it because it affects the *Times*. *The Poste* is owned by The Corp."

"So far I can follow."

"Now, *The Poste* has used data from another company of The Corp for an article."

"I remember hearing about that. I don't have all the details of the terms The Corp had with the Department of Justice, but I know one centerpiece was the Chinese walls obligation: no sharing of data between the companies."

Roberta crossed her arms. "I'm not a lawyer, but as far as I understand, said company had a data transfer agreement with another company and they had one with *The Poste*."

"They can't win. If they do, any data will be shareable within the two conglomerates with no boundaries. There are contracts between most of The Holding's companies—somewhere there is always a link."

"That's what I mean. This man... what was his name again?"

"Dennings. Jude Dennings."

"I think I've heard that name before. Your Jude Dennings simply needs to sign agreements with others and your data is almost public. It's as simple as that—or it goes through three different companies, being a little stirred or shaken, and there is your access. It's like data laundering."

August let his shoulders drop. "So, I have been deceived. Fooled."

"I'm sorry I brought it up, it was just a thought."

"No, that's your profession." He shook his head. "I'm not yet sure if I should be proud that my gut feeling was right, or if I should be angry at not having listened to it." August shrugged. "What does it matter? They do what they want anyway."

"You still have the IT ticket that proves the issue."

He looked up. "Right, I have to follow up on that one again."

The waitress set the tables around them for lunch. August looked at his watch. "Jeez, I lost track of the time." He jumped up and grabbed his bag. "Sorry, I have to run."

"No worries, I have to run too."

"Don't forget dinner tomorrow night?"

"I won't."

"See you tomorrow then. And don't forget: Triple-Ts win at last."

#

Niklas

Niklas had woken up early this morning. He had a headache and his eyes were dry, typical for spending the night on that filthy sofa in the office. *Damn air conditioning. Damn weekend shifts— especially this one.* He looked at his screen. The job was 90% done and there was one hour until shift change. He went to the little bathroom to freshen up. They had been too stingy to put a shower in here; the vapor could compromise the servers, they had said. *Bullshit. They just didn't want to invest a cent before moving the whole facility out to the new set-up.* It had been a crap weekend and he felt like crap.

When he came back he had a new message on his Comm-Dongle. He grabbed his VR glasses and was about to throw them across the room, but he finished the move without letting them go. Niklas put them back on the desk and opened the chat window.

'I assume you executed what we discussed. Confirm.'

He waited for a second and a second message appeared.

'I'm waiting.'

Niklas rolled out the keyboard. *Damn deactivated voice command.* Still standing, he typed, 'Confirmed.'

One second later a new message appeared. 'Including the back door?'

Niklas sat down and pinged the project leader a simple 'Yes'. If he had to talk to him for one more minute this weekend he would throw up or kill somebody. No answer came back.

#

At 8AM Niklas could finally leave when his supervisor, John, arrived. Back home he had his weekend-shift Monday routine: shower, coffee and back to bed for another nap. He slept longer than usual, and the buzz of a new message woke him up; August was asking if he wanted to come over tomorrow for dinner with a guest. Niklas picked up his Comm-Dongle and called back.

"Hey mate, I hope I didn't wake you up." August's voice sounded upbeat for an ordinary office day.

Niklas rubbed his eyes and sat up. "No worries. Coffee this afternoon?"

"Sure, but aren't you off today?"

"I need to tell you something. Does two o'clock work for you?" He gazed over at his ancient radio alarm clock. The green figures said 11.30AM.

"Two is fine. See you later then. Wait, you are coming tomorrow night, right?"

"Of course."

"Great. See you later."

Niklas fell back into the bed and watched the ceiling. His thoughts were playing hide-and-seek. *Back-door entry, greatest sin of a programmer, need an insurance policy.* Thoughts swirled round his head. Every time he tried to catch one, it escaped again until his eyelids felt heavy and he closed his eyes.

#

The buzz tone of his Comm-Dongle woke him up again. It was a message from August that he would be fifteen minutes late. Niklas rubbed his eyes and jumped out of the bed. It was already 1.45PM. Niklas rushed out.

August was waiting outside the Lakeshore with the two cups of coffee.

"Sorry for being late, I fell asleep again." Niklas ran his hand through his hair and got his quadruple espresso.

"No worries, how was your weekend?"

"Dark and dusty. Three more weekends down there and I'll turn into a Morlock."

"Or a troll—you can be my guest troll tomorrow night." August chuckled, but Niklas only answered with a grunt.

"What guest are you expecting tomorrow night? Is it informal or do I need to prepare a speech and get my tux out for dry cleaning?"

August was beaming. "I told you about the interview with the journalist."

"At least a dozen times," Niklas sighed. "What a waste of time. How boring, having all the questions and answers censored. But what does that have to do with tomorrow night?"

"Well, it turned out to be an awesome time. She's a Triple-T."

Niklas opened his eyes. "You haven't told her anything you shouldn't, right?"

"Nothing really secret and it was off the record..."

Niklas threw his hands into the air.

August frowned. "What?"

"What did you tell her?" Niklas' eyes remained on August for a second and then he shook his head and turned around, looking out to the lake. *I'm too tired for this shit.* "Let me guess," Niklas turned back to August and looked him in the eye. "You told her about the SURE data exchange, didn't you?"

"What's bad about that?"

"What's bad?" Niklas threw his hands into the air again and almost threw away his coffee cup. "Everything! Everything. She's a journalist, for Christ's sake. Even without a recorder she will remember this. You have no clue where she will use it, or when. This could hit you from behind in ten years. Ladies and gentlemen, here's a dead man walking."

August was looking down at his coffee cup as if the answers would be in there. "I had a good feeling about her. She's a Triple-T."

Niklas took two deep breaths. "You're a nice guy, but sometimes you're just naive. Brilliant and strategic in one moment, just to overthrow everything one moment later. All you can do is hope you're right about her."

"But you'll come tomorrow?" August looked like a beaten dog in that moment. "Come on, you can't let me down. Please, you have to come. You're like family."

Niklas wiggled his head. "Sure, but only to protect you from yourself." He took a breath and closed his eyes for a second.

"So, what happened that you got out of bed for a coffee?"

"My weekend shift was miserable."

"More miserable than usual?" August straightened.

"Far worse. They wanted me to put stuff in that's more dark red than orange, but I didn't have a handle to say no. They had the approval from the chief architect as well as the program manager."

"What was it?"

"Doesn't matter, but they explicitly didn't want the changes to be logged."

August whistled, surprised. "Now that's what I call a red flag."

"I didn't do it. I told them I did, but I created a sub-routine that logged it separately."

"Good boy. By the way, you remember the issue with the sign-off dates in the future? I opened a ticket so I could always say that I assumed it was an IT glitch. Guess what answer came back today? Ticket closed, with the comment 'Dates will not be in the future by tomorrow.' Obviously sometime in the future the signatures will not in the future anymore!"

"Morons." Niklas looked back again over the lake with squinted eyes. "You always need to have insurance." After a while he asked, "Do you ever wonder when this will all go?"

August followed Niklas' stare. "This?"

"We, humanity, the US, big business—just all this."

"It won't." August shrugged. "We'll muddle on like we always do. My dad used to say one man can learn, but mankind never will. I like to think that mankind gets better, but it's for each and every one of us to carry the torch and hand it over to our kids."

"We're just small fishes in this pond. The real big ones, like your Dennings or my program manager, they want to improve themselves and don't mind abusing the system."

"They might, but look at their predecessors. In the end, they all got caught. They couldn't stop and eventually their greed took them too far and they fell. Those guys will be no different."

"You seriously believe that?" Niklas turned back to August. "The list of those who got away with it is only superseded by the list of their victims." He shook his head. "I tell you: data. It's their Achilles' heel."

"No way. Blockchain is unbreakable. You can't alter data—the link between the data packets can't be changed."

Niklas had stopped listening and was again looking out over the lake to the Adirondack Mountains on the other shore. *Blockchain is only as strong as its weakest link.* For the first time he felt disconnected from his friend. *This is not about blockchain—why don't you see it?* "A storm is coming, don't you think?"

CHAPTER THREE

The Moon

Olivia – July 23 – 4 Years to Day 0 (Burlington, VT)

Olivia wasn't at all happy about her husband's spontaneous dinner invitation. *Is it too much to ask to involve me beforehand?* He had told her in the evening that she shouldn't treat this like a formal invitation; this Roberta would be happy to have a nice, small family dinner.

Well, she had thought, *let's test that.*

In the morning, Olivia rushed through the house, making sure it was clean, and through the grocery store in only three hours. At 11AM she grabbed her bag and her e-reader and left for Lakeshore coffee shop. Olivia often went there to read a book, watch people or enjoy the view of the lake. The coffee shop was busy, but she was able to get a table at the window. The book wasn't too enthralling, so she switched off her table's privacy mode and watched people out of the corners of her eyes, the e-reader still in front of her as a decoy.

Two businessmen on the sofa behind Olivia were engaged in a cramped conversation. Olivia could hear every word. It seemed they hadn't realized that their privacy mode wasn't working properly; one of them had put his jacket over one of the noise distributors.

"When's the last time you called Mom?"

The other guy mumbled something she didn't understand, but it clearly wasn't the answer the other one had wanted to hear. He was rebuked. Olivia guessed the brothers to be about five years apart.

"Have you only come here to tell me I should call Mom?"

Snap. Olivia looked down and bit on her lips in order not to smile. She risked a peek to see how they looked. The older brother was taller. *He is actually quite good looking,* Olivia thought, *but too boring. Too straight-backed and not enough chest.* She turned back and noticed that she could see them in one of the mirrors on the wall. *This is better than theater.* Both were wearing business uniforms: black suits, shirts with thin blue stripes and blueish ties with diagonal stripes. The younger brother was a little more extravagant with his shiny shoes, which he wiggled on the side of the table, and the silver and lapis lazuli cufflinks. *I'll call them Gordon and Gecko.* This time she smiled.

"No, I wanted to chat with you because I might switch to your company," said Gordon, the older of the two.

"Really?" replied Gecko with the excitement of a New England winter.

"They offered me the management of all US data centers, except one in the Midwest."

Gecko sat up. Olivia couldn't see it clearly, but she had the feeling he had put on an alert face.

"I wouldn't take that offer."

"Why not?"

"For once, trust your little brother."

"I need a little more than that. This is an opportunity to get away from restructuring projects where everything ends up with people getting laid off. I have a little son now and a lot of bills to pay."

Gecko peeked left and right. "I know—just trust me."

Gordon didn't reply, so Gecko leaned forward and continued with a lower voice. "I am part of this project. I tell you, this will change the shape of the world." Now his voice got a thrilled undertone. "All communication is encrypted to the highest standards and we have regular meetings with the FBI, CIA and CybDef."

"So what?"

"Let me finish. At the beginning it was about a new data center, nothing special. But when I got promoted to project manager, I got involved in the master plan. We are merging all data centers and outsourcing the whole service to a new company. But here's the thing: it's a joint venture. The Corp is doing the same. Can you imagine the billions of savings? That's why you shouldn't take the job: they will need you to lay off the people in those data centers."

Gordon shrugged, but it looked more like dropping his shoulders. "That means nothing. They will still need somebody to manage that new data center, and in my experience it will still be in The Holding. I've changed companies more than I've changed jobs."

"They won't, that's the thing. The data center will be fully automated with only minimal manual intervention. It is the first of its kind entirely based on blockchain."

Now Gordon really did let his shoulders drop. "And where would this data center be?"

"One is in the Midwest," said Gecko, proud and ignoring his brother's misery. "But there are three other hubs where the data is mirrored. With this set-up we even might skip back-ups and archiving. It's not yet through the steering committee, but imagine the money we would save alone with that." Gecko's smirk turned into a grin. "One other hub will be in the Australian desert, a third one in the Swiss Alps in an old military bunker, but you'll never guess where the fourth will be." With an arrogant smile he waited for Gordon to guess.

"I'm not in the mood for guessing," Gordon surrendered.

"On the moon. It'll be the first permanent colony outside Earth and we're building it. Fourteen geostationary satellites will ensure that there are always two Earth-based centers in contact with the lunar center, and if they lose connection the satellites can store data for 72 hours. It's perfect." Finally he noticed his brother's mood. "I'm sorry I disappointed you. Actually I shouldn't tell you all this—it's top secret."

With these last words, Gordon erupted, throwing his entire frustration back into his brother's face. "Then why have you told me? Do you have any idea what you've dragged me into? I now have the choice to either report you and kick you out of society or shut up and risk being kicked out myself if they find out."

"Relax. Who would know? We're safe here."

"I have to go," said Gordon and stood up. "Make sure you call Mom."

Gecko stared out at the lake.

Gordon waited for a moment and added, "Fine," before he walked away.

"You should be grateful I saved you," Gecko threw after his brother. He got up and left as well.

Olivia was wondering who would pick up the tab. A minute later, she lowered the e-reader and looked around. Nobody else seemed to have been listening; the privacy function had apparently only leaked to her table. *I have to tell August,* she thought. *He will be flabbergasted.*

#

Jenny

Jenny was home drudging at her homework when her mother arrived back from her afternoon out.

"Jenny, are you home? Can you help me with the dinner, please? I'm late," her mom shouted through the house and the intercom echoed it in a decent voice.

Jenny jumped, threw her VR glasses on the table and rushed out of the door, not even taking care to reply to the latest chat from her classmate.

"Mom, there's a reason we have an AI intercom at home," she said when she arrived in the kitchen. "Also, those sticky notes—that's so pre-millennial."

Her mom was already chopping vegetables. "But I love them! They're only two dollars."

Jenny sighed, took one note and stuck it to her forehead.

"Don't mock me." Her mom protested with a smile on her face. "I'm your mother."

Jenny smirked. "What can I do?"

"Can you set the table? Over there I've got decorations." Her mom pointed to some paper napkins and a plastic tablecloth.

"Let me guess, two dollars each." Jenny unpacked the first napkin pack. "Who's the guest Daddy invited?"

"Roberta, a *New York Times* journalist."

"Really!? Can Eduard come too? Please! He would love to get insights for his writing." Jenny felt her face prickling. "I'll give him a buzz." She turned around and left the kitchen.

"We still have to talk about that, young lady," she heard her mom shout after her as she ran upstairs to her Comm-Dongle. By the time she came back down, her mom had already prepared the food and was about to decorate the table. "That was quite a phone call." Her mom tilted her head and, despite the funny comment, she didn't smile.

Jenny lost her smile for a second as well. "Edu had *something* he needed to tell me."

"And that couldn't wait until tonight, I guess." This time her mom smiled mildly.

Jenny pouted. "I'm sorry, I might have lost track of time."

"But your timing is perfect to decorate the table while I sit down and take a break and watch you." Her mom's smile took on a smirky touch.

They went into the dining room. Jenny picked up the decorations from where she had left them and her mom sat down.

"Don't you want to tell me what happened at your party the other day?" The smile went from her face again.

"Nothing happened. We were just tired and fell asleep."

"We still need to talk. I've noticed how you've changed since you've started dating him. You've let your hair grow, you're wearing earrings and you're using my make-up—and your eyes sparkle violet." Her mom paused for a moment. "We told you to disable pink. It's dangerous to show that you're attracted to somebody, especially for girls."

Jenny pretended she had not heard and tried to concentrate on the decorations.

"Look at me."

The change in her mom's voice made her look up.

"I know how this feels, I've been there. I just don't want you to rush into anything."

"Mooom, please." The prickling sensation in her face was back and her ears felt hot.

"I'm serious, honey. I understand how it feels to be in love for the first time. Everything is different and nothing else matters anymore. You want to soak up every moment and never let go again."

"What's wrong with that?" Jenny's back stiffened up.

"Nothing, you should enjoy it. But don't forget the future for it. There are things you can't get back."

"I know that, Mom, I really do." Her arms felt feeble. "And I promise you I won't do anything stupid." She had to put the napkins unfolded back on the table.

Her mom stood up and gave her a hug and Jenny sank in her arms. "I know, my love, but I have to say it anyway. I can't help it," Olivia said after a moment and looked into her daughter's eyes.

Jenny put on a smile, but it came out weaker than intended.

"There are so many things I have to tell you, mistakes I made that I don't want you to have to go through too," Olivia continued. "Even if you don't want to hear it right now, but in a healthy relationship you do have fights..."

"Not that story again," said Jenny, laughing again. "I've heard it a dozen times. I even heard both sides. It gets bigger every time I hear it—the amount spent on shopping grew from one to sixteen grand, and the time Dad spent camping in the woods increased from a weekend to an entire week. And all for what?"

"Nothing. Old stories." Her mom was laughing too. "I guess you could write a book about it."

She let go of Jenny and put the appetizers on the dining table.

#

Dad and Niklas were late; they barely arrived before Roberta. Even Eduard had arrived earlier, but it had been a short welcome and Jenny had taken him right up to her room. They had been in the same class in school since first grade. Until two years ago, Eduard had been smaller than Jenny and his brown hair had been shorter than hers. Both had changed after they had started dating and he had grown so fast that now he appeared lanky. Jenny loved that he was taller now, but she didn't like his long hair.

"Leave the door open," shouted her mom from downstairs. Jenny pulled a face, but before she could say anything the AI intercom sounded a beep.

"Daddy is outside," she winked at Eduard. "I put an alert in place—that way I can welcome him every day."

The door went. "Here they are," Jenny heard her mother say, followed by her dad saying, "I'm sorry, honey, I got held up."

"You could have called, my dear."

"It's my fault." That was Niklas' voice. "I needed to get something from my place and I hijacked him. We have no signal out in the old industrial complex and traffic is horrible at that time of the day."

Jenny and Eduard chuckled at Niklas' comment. Jenny's dad had come upstairs to change.

"You always give him a nice excuse," said Olivia, but this time she had laughter in her voice.

"I like Niklas, he's cool," said Eduard to Jenny.

Jenny nodded. The voices softened as they moved over to the kitchen.

"You know," said Jenny with a playful, innocent voice, "Daddy first brought him over when I was nine. I was so in love with his blue eyes."

"Yeah, that happened to me too with my English teacher last year."

Jenny gave Eduard a poke with her elbow. He howled and they both laughed.

"Let's go down," said Jenny. "It'll be fun."

The moment they arrived in the kitchen, the AI intercom voice came on. "One person is at the front of the door." Dad was still changing.

"That must be our guest." Olivia went to the door.

"Hi, Niklas, how are you?" Jenny welcomed him with a hug.

"Same old, same old. But good to see you. Two. Eduard, right?"

"Hello, sir." Eduard shook his hand.

"Jeez! Niklas, please call me Niklas."

"Welcome. I'm Olivia. August will be right with us," they heard Olivia saying. "So, how is the weather in New York?"

The voices were getting closer.

"Very nice. Summer was hot. Many people got heated up though."

"There were some dangerous incidents, I heard."

The voices stopped outside the kitchen.

"I love your house, it's so nice."

"Thank you, we try to keep it a mix between modern and vintage."

The door opened and a woman entered the room. Jenny forgot to breathe for a second. Despite her small posture, Jenny had the feeling a giant had entered the room. She wasn't able to articulate in her mind what it was—the grey eyes, the wiry body or the vivid and exploring air. She wasn't able to articulate anything. Jenny glanced at Eduard and he stood there gazing at Roberta. Eduard had had so many questions before, but now he didn't dare to ask even one. Her mom apparently shared a mutual understanding with Roberta. They were jumping from one topic to another. After talking about the recent uptick of assaults in New York City they discussed how the company security of The Holding and The Corp were taking over more and more police work, but only protecting their own employees.

In the meantime they had sat down at the dinner table, enjoying the snacks Olivia had prepared.

Eduard was following the chat like a crouching panther, waiting for a chance to jump in and hijack the conversation. Niklas leaned back and observed the talk. He wasn't frowning or giving any other sign of disapproval, but his fake smiles indicated that he wasn't happy. Jenny wondered why that was.

Jenny's dad joined them three hop-on, hop-off topics later and welcomed Roberta heartily. Now there were three people talking in front of a three-person audience, until her mom tried to involve Jenny in the discussion.

"Jenny, you're so silent."

"It's ok," Jenny replied with a chortle. "When grown-ups talk, we kids listen with rapt attention."

"And what's your excuse?" her dad threw at Niklas.

"The same," he replied and added to Roberta, "They adopted me at twenty-five."

The laughter loosened them up a little and the kids now participated more actively. Eduard got his chance to pepper Roberta with questions.

#

As the evening went on, the mood got familiar. The appetizers had been devoured and Jenny's mom had brought out the main course: pizza and a large bowl of mixed salad. "Your dad said to just put on a simple family dinner," she explained with a smirk.

It had gotten dark outside and the conversation around the hot New York summer had picked up again.

Roberta sighed. "It's a pity the *Times* moved their offices to Greenwich, but it got too dangerous in the city. Even before the recent uptick of assaults, I had to take a limousine to work. Imagine, they produce the *New York Times* in Connecticut."

"Tell me, how is it at the *Times* at the moment?" asked Olivia.

Roberta chuckled. "What you actually want to ask me is, why has the *Times* deteriorated so much?"

Jenny's dad closed his mouth in slow motion and swallowed the question he wanted to ask. It was silent in the room. For a moment Jenny thought she heard the TV in their neighbor's house. *Finally, somebody who talks real.* She glanced up at the others; her parents gaped at Roberta, and Niklas squinted.

After a moment, Roberta snorted with laughter. "Guys, you should see your faces."

Mom and Dad still didn't seem convinced; only Niklas' mouth twitched at the corners.

Jenny's mother regained her voice first. "I hope you don't want me to sign a non-disclosure agreement. Seems I have to get my questions approved by August otherwise he'll have a heart attack someday." She winked at him as if she was authorized to speak freely now.

Roberta laughed. "That's a good one. But back to your question—the answer is simple." Her voice changed to a serious tone. "The Holding needed a PR department and buying the *Times* was the cheapest solution. The question is, what happened to the ethics of The Holding?"

"See, Roberta," said Jenny's dad, "it's the same as the Catholic Church. Most members are good-willed, but there are those who are only following their narcissistic targets. They don't care about any ethical or legal boundaries. But most of the time it's just human error. You don't know how many times we detect a violation and in the end it turns out to be an employee who wasn't aware of the rule or who mistyped something."

"Exactly," Jenny heard herself saying, "but as long as the management and leadership concepts focus on policy and regulation, an employee only has to decide whether he complies or not. He will never have to think about what is right or wrong. On the contrary, the companies and even the government don't want people to think in terms of right or wrong because that could lead to disobedience. Free will is their enemy."

Her mom's face froze and Jenny swallowed hard. But then she clenched her jaw. *No, I am right.*

Roberta eyebrows twitched before she answered into the silence. "You have to watch what terms you use. If you say that out loud in public, they might push you into the anarchy corner. Social media is powerful and unforgiving. It's like a witch hunt—once you have the tag, you won't be able to get rid of it."

"That's exactly the problem." *Why are they allowed to say what they want and I'm not?* Heat was flushing through Jenny's body. "Social media is abused for bullying and defaming. The moment the internet was integrated into the Telecommunication Act, the carriers and the social networks with them were not liable for the content anymore. But who changed the law? It wasn't our generation, but we have to live with it."

"Every generation deserves a McCarthy." Niklas picked up his glass and sipped.

Roberta disregarded Niklas' comment. "No need to be angry with me," she said mildly. "I've been fighting stupidity and ignorance my whole life."

"I'm sorry, I didn't mean to..." Jenny turned to Eduard. "Can't you say something as well? We discussed this."

"Enough, Jenny," said her mom and added towards Roberta, "I have to apologize."

"No need to. Truth is always welcome—it's the foundation of what we believe in." She looked at Jenny. "But I'm worried that you talk like this in the open. I've seen too many friends go under because they were not smart."

Again, an oppressive silence lay over the table.

"Who wants to have dessert or coffee?" asked Jenny's dad and slapped his leg. "Jenny, will you help me?"

"I can help too," said Eduard quickly and stood up.

"You can help me here to clean up the table a little," said Olivia.

Jenny looked down, but she felt their eyes on her. Eduard squeezed her hand.

"Jenny?" Her dad was waiting at the door.

It took Jenny a moment to get up and then she shuffled behind her dad into the kitchen. "I'm sorry, I didn't mean to—"

"Don't be," her dad interrupted her. "In this house you are always allowed your opinion."

Jenny tried a shy smile.

"But do be sorry for alienating your family and friends—for what? For nothing. If you express your opinion, even to support somebody, be smart. Choose your words wisely. Never appear angry. And remember, your eyes sell you out with those contact lenses." He pointed to her eyes and raised his eyebrows. "Right now they're orange, which means aggravation, as I understand it."

"But that's newspeak, Daddy," replied Jenny, ignoring his warning about the contact lenses.

"No, it isn't. Don't say it the wrong way round, but say it non-offensively. Always remember: you never know the other person's pain."

"I'm sorry, Dad. Please don't be mad anymore."

Her dad hugged her. "I never was."

When they went back into the dining room, they found a lively discussion going on between Eduard and Roberta about the different professions around writing and the multiple ways to get there. Olivia winked at Jenny and her dad.

Jenny remembered the rest of the evening as very nice, with lots of laughter. No toxic topics were touched on anymore. When Roberta left she thanked them for the wonderful evening and the chance to meet a genuine family. They all promised to stay in contact and Niklas was nice enough to give her a ride to the hotel.

#

When Jenny came back into the house after she had said goodbye to Eduard, she heard her parents talking in the kitchen. They were talking randomly, but then her mom seemed to get very excited about something.

"I almost forgot," she started, "you won't guess what I overheard today in the mall. It's a big thing."

Jenny couldn't help but sit down in the living room, switch the TV on mute and listen to the conversation. She knew they would stop if she joined them in the kitchen, and it was an exciting story her mom was telling. It almost sounded like an espionage thriller. Jenny was fascinated, but it seemed like her dad wasn't. He interrupted several times, asking what exactly the men had said or if they had mentioned the company's name.

He sighed when she had finished. "You realize I have to report this to our Integrity Department? This is a major breach of protocol."

"I didn't think of that. Do you really have to?"

He paused for a moment before he sighed again. "Yes. I'm still a senior manager of The Holding and I have to do the right thing."

Jenny's mom didn't like that; the excessive silence afterwards told Jenny everything.

CHAPTER FOUR

Jude Dennings

August – July 26 – 4 Years to Day 0 (Burlington, VT)

First thing on Wednesday August reported the issue. There was an online form to be filled out, followed by several calls from compliance departments around the globe trying to get to the heart of the issue.

It took up half of his day and he was happy when he thought it was over, but it wasn't. Two days later he received a rather cryptic invitation to appear thirty minutes later in person at a secured meeting room, with no further details than 'integrity reporting'. August knew he had stirred something up, but when he saw the invitation his throat felt dry—they wouldn't dare to fire him, would they?

No way, that would be against the non-retaliation policy. He shook off the thought when something else came to his mind. *I'll be late—it will take me at least twenty minutes to get down there and through the security.* August took the glove and swooshed the report and additional papers and notes onto the big screen. His tongue licked his lips while he flipped through the pages. He checked the time, grabbed his Comm-Dongle and left.

He arrived two minutes late. The guard at the security checkpoint sneered at him; his bald head, short neck and broad shoulders made him look like he was built out of toy blocks. *Niklas is working somewhere around here,* thought August when he walked down the hallway, passing other conference rooms. Through the milky glass he could see that one conference room he passed was occupied, but he couldn't recognize anybody inside.

The guard guided him to a room with clear glass. "Wait here," he snarked and closed the door. The clear glass became translucent like the other conference rooms.

"Why does perceived power make people so unfriendly?" August said to himself as he sat down.

The room was bathed in a dark grey light and when he had been standing it appeared dim. Now that he was sitting, the indirect light from the behind the handrail around three-quarters of the room made it appear bright. He stood up and it appeared dark again.

The guard opened the door again and another man entered the room. A cool draft accompanied him as if somebody had increased the air conditioning. With a motionless face he nodded to the security guard, who closed the door behind him. He turned to August and put on a smile.

"Now we finally meet in person."

August was left to guess who he was. His slender figure didn't fill his expensive suit. The missing tie and the suspenders gave him an elegant look that would have fit more in Wall Street in the 1980s than here, if the rosy cheeks had not broken the image.

With those cheeks he looked a little like he had grown up too early, but his rimy eyes corrected this impression.

He walked towards August and shook his hand.

"I'm Jude. Jude Dennings."

August tried to smile but it came out wrong. *They must have retouched the cheeks in the company photos.* "Mr. Dennings, nice to meet you." *Mr. Dennings? How stupid.*

"Jude. I insist. Please, take a seat."

August sat down. Jude sat down across from him and looked at him for just a little too long.

"Did they already offer you a coffee or a water?"

"No." August's dry throat didn't allow him to say more.

Jude raised his eyebrows. "Would you like one?"

August nodded. Jude nodded as well—slower than August—and set up the same smile he had had when he entered. It was slightly out of phase; it happened a microsecond before he said anything or after he finished talking, as if he wanted to give a signal that the other one was now allowed to talk. Jude must have pressed a button. The door opened and the guard came back; this time he was friendliness personified.

"You must be wondering why I invited you to this meeting, August," said Jude after the guard had left again.

August swallowed. "I was informed that the subject is the reported integrity violation."

"That is true, in a certain sense."

"Everything I know is already in the report or has been discussed in several phone calls. I don't have more details about the second person." August's voice was almost shaking.

"We took care of the people involved. Now we have to clean up the rest."

The door opened again and the guard came back with August's coffee and a paper for Dennings.

Who still uses paper? thought August.

"Thanks, Frank," said Dennings without visible emotion. After the guard had left, Dennings studied the paper and continued without looking up. "They got new assignments within the project that they couldn't refuse—in a remote area in Africa, with fewer contact points outside the company. We still have a lot of open positions there. You have to understand, August, we can't let the project be compromised further."

August's throat went dry again and he swallowed.

"I need you to sign this non-disclosure agreement." He stood up and put the paper in front of August. Every movement seemed controlled—too carefully controlled.

"I understand." August read through the paper. It was short for a non-disclosure agreement.

"I'm sure you do. As you're involved now, we would like to offer you a chair on the expert committee of our project. OneHub—that's the name of the project—needs to have constant input from senior subject-matter experts like yourself who understand the strategic implications."

The word 'offer' made August look up from the paper. "That sounds very interesting, but I don't think the workload of my current position would allow additional responsibilities."

"I have to apologize, August, I might have made myself unclear." Again that out-of-phase smile. "This would be a full-time position. You would still work out of Burlington, if you wish, but it would include 20% travelling, I'm afraid. And you would be promoted to Managing Director, which of course would include a 50% raise, as far as I understand."

August inhaled sharply. "I'm flattered, but I would need to discuss this with my wife, of course." His heartbeat was dashing and his brain was feverishly calculating. *That's ten years earlier debt-free.*

"Of course. Speaking of her, we need you to ask her to sign the non-disclosure agreement as well. I'm sure she will understand. One day I would like to meet her."

"I will ask her."

"Thank you, August. I appreciate it."

August finished reading the agreement after a minute; he was used to them, but he wasn't sure how to sell it to Olivia.

"I don't have a pen."

Jude handed him a black pen with a diamond at the end. It felt heavy and the tip looked as if it was made of gold. August wasn't used to signing with his bare hands anymore and his signature came out a little off.

The guard appeared in the door.

"I have to go," said Jude, "my helicopter should be here any minute." He stood up and shook August's hand. "That perk would also come with the new position. We really could use somebody like you."

"I'll let you know by tomorrow."

"I'm sure you will. And don't worry about your current manager. He will not oppose this change."

August frowned briefly. "You already talked to him?"

"Of course not. He's not part of OneHub." Again he put on his out-of-phase smile. "We will stay in contact," Jude said while walking to the door.

After he had left, August dropped back into the chair. *I have to get back to the office,* he thought, but for a minute or two he sat there like he was paralyzed. *Ten years less!*

A draft of cool air drew him out of his state. He slowly stood up and walked out, without having even touched his coffee.

When he got back to his floor he was surprised that it was still daylight, but then he realized that it was not even lunchtime. August would have loved to get support from Niklas, but he couldn't tell him anything without violating the non-disclosure agreement he had just signed. He started to work down his task list, but everything felt meaningless. Why was he still doing this when his successor could do it all? It was as if he was working remotely, directing his fingers from somewhere else.

#

'Coffee? N.'

The buzz of the message brought August back to reality. He looked at the clock. *Three already?* August hesitated a moment. Eventually he texted back 'Sure', but he knew he had to be cautious.

#

Niklas

It was drizzling when August arrived. Niklas waited with the coffee in their usual place, just three yards further up where they had cover.

"What's up, mate?"

"The usual." August shrugged half-heartedly and suppressed the need to sputter everything out.

"You look as if you've seen a ghost," Niklas smirked.

August tried to smile. "Nah, just tired."

"I got an e-mail today with the updated list of the *chosen ones* and I saw your name. Hence, welcome over the Wall. But how come?"

August still looked puzzled, but he didn't say a word.

Niklas guessed that his friend was trying to grasp a thought. "Jeez, they must have scared you." He raised his eyebrows. "Ok, now, for the record, I'm also on OneHub. You signed the non-disclosure agreement today, right?"

"Oh boy. You too?" August frowned. "You never told me."

"Well, guess why. But I definitely left you enough bread-crumbs. Now, what's your job on the project?"

"There were other reasons they wanted me to sign the non-disclosure agreement—"

"We refer to that agreement as the 'mute button'."

August didn't jump on the joke and Niklas' smile yielded to a frown.

"I've been offered a new job, completely new, giving up my current one. On the 'expert committee', whatever that is." August's shoulders dropped in an attempt to shrug. "It doesn't feel like I have much of a choice though."

"Yeah right, the expert committee wouldn't leave me with a lot of choice either. Man, that's a great job and a huge jump in your career."

"That's not what I mean. I'm not sure if I'll lose my job if I don't accept."

Now Niklas shrugged. "Senior management problem."

August told Niklas the whole story, from Olivia overhearing the conversation, to him reporting it, to the meeting with Jude and the job offer.

"Now I understand." Niklas looked out into the rain. "The name of that 'Gecko' is Michal. He was my project manager. The one who had me working my weekend shifts and putting that dark red stuff into the system. Remember? Two days ago we were informed that he would lead the local operations in the African data center, somewhere in the Congo." He blew out air through his mouth. "I wasn't aware that Jude Dennings was over the Wall too. He doesn't appear on any of the lists."

"You probably only get a part of the list, or he's above the Wall."

"Tomorrow the new project manager will be announced. Hope he's a little more open to my concerns."

"What concerns?" August tilted his head.

"There are major risks in this project."

"I couldn't agree more. The project is a tremendously ambitious—"

"Not for the project, for the company." Niklas interrupted him. "It's the design, it's flawed. These management guys made decisions without understanding the risks."

"What decisions?"

"For example, abandoning back-ups, or assigning data centers the same priority without having a clear master. That's like throwing a dice to decide which data is correct."

August wiggled his head. "I've read a recent paper from an MIT professor and he predicts these changes to happen over the next few years." He smiled. "Maybe we're the *old guys*."

"Let me guess, Prof. Yilmez, right? He knows it will happen because he's on the expert committee as well. They want him to make these vague predictions publicly for PR. But soon you can discuss these topics in person with him."

"Really? Who else is on the board?" August's eyes got an excited glow.

"He's the only one I know by name, but there are people from the military, NASA, the FBI, the NSA and all the rest of it. So-called specialists, but if you ask me the only real specialist on that board would be you." Niklas poked August to get his attention back. "Back to my little issue called the 'design flaw'."

"Yeah, I'm not sure if it's that flawed after all. Ultimately the solution won't be as bad as you might think. They will test everything and if something doesn't work, they'll fix it."

Niklas shook his head. "It's not a theory. I know it for a fact."

#

Olivia

Olivia knew something was going on when August got out of the car and trudged over from the garage through the rain. She was sitting on the porch with a hot tea and her e-reader; she loved sitting there, listening to the drizzle. He walked as if there was weight on his shoulders and he didn't care if he got wet in the drizzle. She looked at the clock on her e-reader: 6PM. Jenny would soon be home, but they still had some minutes to talk.

August shook his head. "Later."

She pressed her lips together and looked after him. It got worse as August didn't speak a word during dinner. He wolfed down the pasta, but Olivia couldn't eat over two forkfuls. More than once she tried to start a conversation, but he didn't engage if he answered at all. In the end she only shot him concerned looks, but he either didn't notice or ignored them. Even Jenny seemed to sense something; she looked at her parents in turns and disappeared right after dinner with a superficial excuse.

"What's wrong, honey?" asked Olivia after Jenny had left.

August blew air through his pressed lips.

"Nothing's wrong, not really. It's actually a good thing. I just don't trust it."

"What thing? You talk in riddles." Her stomach churned.

"That report I handed in about the things you heard at the mall, it has implications. The two guys got deployed to the data center in Africa and I had to sign a non-disclosure agreement today." He bit on his lips. "They also want me to have you sign one."

"Africa? Good lord." Olivia shook her head. "I don't like that. Not that I would pass this around, but I'm not even an employee and I don't know what I'll get into." She looked out of the window. It was still raining and drops were rolling down the glass. She turned back to him. "But if you want me to, of course I will."

"Thank you, honey." August smiled before his face went dark again. "There's something else. They offered me a job, a phenomenal one."

"That's a bribe," said Olivia quickly and paused afterwards as if her brain wanted to put what she had just said into perspective. "They must be terrified you'll share something—or I will."

"It feels like a trap. This offer is too good to be true, but the honey is sweet. It's a Managing Director position with a 50% raise. That also means less working in a hamster wheel." He bit on the insides of his cheeks. "I'd have to travel 20% though."

"That is an insane offer, I agree with you. But I don't like the travelling part; I always hate when you're away."

"And I don't like that I can't go back to my old job—Jude made that clear in his speech." August jumped up and paced back and forth in the kitchen. "And even more I don't like being threatened with being sent to Africa—"

"With *what*?" Olivia gasped for air for a second.

August's shoulders dropped. "Not directly, but—" He stopped himself from talking for a moment. "I don't like not having a choice."

"You always have a choice, August. We can live in a smaller house—"

"Jenny won't go to college, and don't even start with the student loans." August clenched his teeth. "I don't want her to end up like us—she's a kid, soon in college, and we're still paying our own student loans."

Olivia felt a little irritated, but August's help-seeking eyes calmed her down. "She will understand."

"She won't. I can see her red eyes."

Olivia knew he was right. She would be mad, at least until she understood how crushing the system can be, but eventually she would understand. *The system*. Her stomach crumbled and a bit of bile came up, giving Olivia a bitter taste in her mouth. "Why don't we leave? Just go away. Start over somewhere else. There must be a country in this world that lets you breathe. China maybe."

The begging disappeared from his eyes. "The risk is too high of us losing everything, everything we fought for." He sat down again and looked at her. "Why not play the game for a while? Just for two, three years. We'll put the additional 50% aside and see how this works out."

Olivia lowered her eyes and tried to control her breath. "Will the offer still stand even if I don't sign the agreement?"

"Not sure, but what are my options? And I don't like you being dragged into this."

"I'm already in it. We all are." She looked up again after another deep breath. "I'll sign it."

He nodded slowly and she could see a glimpse of relief in his eyes.

"I like the idea of saving the additional money and getting out of our debts earlier. We might even be debt-free when you retire."

August stood up again and took her into his arms. She could feel him letting go of all his worries. Olivia closed her eyes; she would catch him like she always did.

"I am so lucky to have you. You are the most wonderful wife a man could wish for."

"I'm lucky to have you." Olivia opened her eyes. "Oh, have you seen the *New York Times*?" She stood up and detached the e-pad from the fridge. "It's hilarious. They used a picture of you that's at least five years old."

"The interview is out already?" August raised his eyebrows. "I had no time to read or listen to any news today."

Olivia activated her swooshing ring and brought up the *Times* on the e-pad.

August read through the article. "I'm glad they didn't use the one from my corporate ID card. I look like a criminal on that one."

Olivia gave her husband a nudge, but she was glad to see a little wit returning to his eyes.

August raised his eyebrows. "I never said that." The wit was gone again.

"What?" Olivia looked at the e-pad.

"I said that there is always a risk and that absolute safety is unaffordable. That's why we also put great efforts into back-ups and contingency plans. This was even Holding-approved, but look what they turned it into. Here." He pointed to the sentence he was talking about.

"'Past systems are always a risk,'" Olivia read loud, "'but we have smart people continuously improving system security, and I can assure you IT will soon see a revolution in security.'" She frowned at August. "What's wrong with that?"

"Well, it's not wrong per se. I mean, it's the usual babble, but I didn't say that."

"Anything else they changed?"

"Yes, here they changed me saying that we would never share data with government agencies or other Holding companies into a stupid standard phrase that 'we can assure you we operate within legal and moral boundaries'."

Olivia's eyes felt dry. She had to blink twice to get rid of the sensation. "I would never have thought this of Roberta. Why would she do this?"

August chuckled with a scary undertone. "This has the handwriting of The Holding. I'm sure she wasn't involved. Let me call her."

"Are you sure? If she is involved it might cause more issues."

"You're right. I shouldn't call. Not because this might be her doing, but because I think the moment I signed the nondisclosure agreement they added my office phone and my Comm-Dongle to the critical employee list." He clenched his jaw. "You know what that means, right?"

"No, what's that?"

"They scan for buzzwords and set-up alerts. I have to watch what I say on the phone from now on."

"Is that legal?" Olivia shook her head in disbelief.

"It's their phone and I signed."

"But you could still call her from our home phone."

"That would even look more suspicious, me calling the *New York Times* from my home communicator to avoid the office phone. And their phone lines will be screened as well."

Olivia sighed, went to the fridge again and got out an open bottle of wine and a beer. She poured the wine into a glass and took a sip.

"I don't like how this job offer is working out. Actually, I wish I had shut up." She crossed her arms in front of her chest.

August shrugged helplessly. "I guess I have to accept tomorrow." He took the beer and looked down at the table in front of him.

CHAPTER FIVE

The Trip

August – August 9 – 4 Years to Day 0 (Burlington, VT)

Two weeks later they received a box of chocolates from Roberta with a card, thanking them again for the nice evening. August was puzzled when Olivia threw the box down in front of him that evening. He opened the box. Half of the chocolates were already gone. He looked at her; she could see him fighting the urge to smile.

She pouted. "They're good. She's still sneaky." She picked up the box again to get another chocolate and frowned.

August tilted his head. "What?"

"It's too heavy." She gave the box back without picking another chocolate.

"Yeah." He lifted the plastic. There were some papers in between the plastic and the cardboard. August got the papers out. "It's my interview!"

"Anything else? A note?"

"No, nothing, just the interview." He frowned. "The right one. See, that's what I said."

August showed the papers to Olivia and she nodded hesitantly. She wasn't sure yet if she should be relieved about Roberta's
honesty or troubled because a company like The Holding changes
interviews.

Later that night August went through the interview again and
showed Olivia three more parts that had been changed. "I knew
it," he said, and switched off the light and turned to the side. Two
minutes later he was snoring quietly.

#

Olivia – March 24, 2042 – 3 Years to Day 0

Afterwards, the Remules didn't hear from Roberta for the entire winter. From time to time Olivia read interviews and articles
by her, always wondering what she had actually handed in. It
seemed a little as if both sides were afraid of getting in touch, but
maybe it was only her own unease.

She took Eduard and Jenny aside one evening for a serious
talk about their opinions, trust and talking openly. They seemed
to understand—at least Eduard did—but Olivia's nervousness just
wouldn't to go away, and it was unusually high the Monday evening Roberta called. August was in the library, which he also used
as his office, when their home communicator rang.

He picked up. "Roberta!"

Olivia rushed into the library.

"Are you around? Where are you calling from?" August was
smiling and he winked at Olivia when she entered the room. She
knew this playing-innocent face too well; he was actually asking if
she was calling from the office or from somewhere secure.

"Oh, you're in New York. So how is spring in the city?" August asked after a moment. "It's nice here. Still a little chilly but lots of sun."

Olivia looked at August's face with rapt attention while he listened.

"You'll be around on the weekend? Come over."

Olivia shook her head to signal August not to invite her over, but he only shrugged his shoulders. He formed the word 'sorry' with his lips.

"Listen, I've got an idea," said August and smiled to Olivia. "There's this cabin in the woods, fifty miles from here, where I go fishing with Niklas from time to time. We could do a weekend trip there."

At least it's not here. Olivia was less worried, but she still frowned at August. Just to be on the safe side, to keep him from having another of his not-thought-through ideas.

"Ok, so we'll get you Friday, 1PM from the airport... Was good to hear from you... We're looking forward to it too. Bye."

Olivia leant on the wall before she spoke again. "I like Roberta and I look forward to seeing her, but this whole circus with secret calls and papers in a box of chocolates gives me the creeps."

"You're right, but it's the best way. The only way to keep up some kind of communication. It's for our own benefit."

"I'm just scared we'll start something that we can't stop."

August stood up and walked over to her. "I promise you that you don't have to worry. I won't let anything impact our lives here at home."

He took her in his arms and she laid her head on his chest. When they were younger she could rest there for hours feeling safe and cherished, but this time it didn't help. Her stomach still felt queasy.

"Trust me." She heard his voice in one ear mixed with his heartbeat in the other.

She looked up. "I trust you, but this is out of our hands."

"I tell you what we can control." He smiled mildly. "We can live our lives and be free here at home, like we always were. We can be cautious not to give anybody reason to make a case against us and we can prepare ourselves for the worst by saving money. And I will do what they want for the time being."

"What if they want something that's illegal?"

"They won't. Even they have to be cautious. With these integrity hotlines and the non-retaliation policy, I always have a way out. We'll be fine. Believe me."

Olivia's unease wouldn't go away, but she pulled herself together. Jenny would soon be home.

"We should invite Niklas and Eduard to the trip," August said when Olivia peeled away from him.

She wiggled her head. "Well, we have to invite Eduard if we want Jenny to come with us."

August smirked.

"I like the idea of the cabin. No eyes, no ears," Olivia added after another deep breath.

"I agree. No announcement of our visitor to the neighborhood watch. I hate that process anyways. They're just nosy, and McLinsky thinks he's King Lionheart in his kingdom."

"More like John Lackland."

They both laughed.

"Sometimes I wonder how we all turned into an army of scared chickens," August said out of the blue as they walked over to the kitchen.

"I know what you mean. Doesn't matter if it's killer rats in LA or the possibility of dog flu jumping over to humans—the haters and trolls on the internet have done their part. And since the attacks on the Palos Verde nuclear plant, every American is a suspect."

"And the McLinskys of this world can play sheriff."

August made coffee and they sat in the kitchen talking, like they had done so often throughout the years. Now that the first moment of fear had passed, Olivia was fine with having a visitor. She was looking forward to it. The unease, however, remained—and her appetite did not return.

#

August – March 28

The rest of the week went by quickly—at least it appeared like that to August, because he could keep his mind occupied with the preparations for the trip. It was exciting compared to the usual routine of preparing the expert committee meeting. Already, after seven months on the project, he was tired of reading thousands of pages of concepts, policies and white papers. And participating in endless preparation calls without making real conclusions or decisions made it even worse. Sometimes it almost seemed to August that the whole purpose of the committee was just to have one, on paper. They were kept out of the decision loop and he asked himself why. That's why August started doing research of his own: retrieving files that were not classified, chatting with people that were over the Wall as well and looking for the scattered impact of the project. It felt like a jigsaw, where you know the outcome but you have to find the pieces and bring them together. August had made it a game. He was looking for infrastructure investments, release plans, office and org-chart changes, but his golden source remained Niklas. From him he knew how and where the project was moving.

On Friday, August left in the early afternoon and when he got home the backpacks were standing ready by the door. He ran upstairs and was back down in jeans and a shirt less than ten minutes later. Olivia was already waiting on him at the door.

"Come on, guys, we have to leave otherwise we'll be hiking in the dark!" he shouted back upstairs.

"Can't we stay another half an hour? I wanted to finish something for school," said Jenny over the house's internal communication system.

"No, honey, we have to leave," he shouted again. "We're looking at a two-hour drive followed by a one-hour hike. And we don't want to keep Roberta waiting at the airport." He heard a suppressed protest from upstairs.

Ten minutes later the kids were ready, the backpacks were in the car and the security alert system was transferred to the neighborhood watch. McLinsky peeked out of his window when they left. *As if he has no cameras,* thought August. *Sometimes I envy Niklas living in that barely surveilled old industrial park.*

They arrived at the airport and August slowed down.

"Over there," Olivia said with a rush in her voice. She pointed to the end of the arrival area.

Roberta was already waiting outside, sitting on the curbside. August didn't recognize her at first in her jeans and with a hiking jacket. Olivia peeked around and checked the side mirrors.

"Everything ok, honey?" he asked while pulling over.

"Of course." She said without looking at him.

August knew this 'of course'; something had made Olivia uncomfortable.

He got out of the car to put Roberta's backpack in the trunk while she squeezed into the back seat next to Jenny and Eduard. Immediately the gaggle and chatter started, as if August had a bunch of kids in his car rather than his family.

Only Olivia remained reserved. Twenty minutes later they were out of the city and on their way.

After a while, August looked at Roberta in the rear mirror and asked, "It's a shame that the Supreme Court decided that data can be shared within a conglomerate like The Holding, isn't it?"

"No shop talk. You promised," threw Olivia in before Roberta could answer.

Roberta nodded. "I agree. This should be a shop-free weekend. Is Niklas coming as well or does he have another weekend shift?"

August glanced at her in the rear mirror again. "No, but he can tell you the story himself. He went ahead this morning to heat the cabin and start the fire."

"Nice to have your own little Swedish servant. Just don't present him with clothes."

August smirked and when he glanced over he saw Olivia's mouth twitching. He felt relieved. In the rear mirror, August saw Jenny throw a questioning glance at Eduard. He shrugged and

Roberta explained the joke. August started to wonder what Roberta's visit was all about.

#

Niklas – (Green River Reservoir, VT)

The cabin was located on the eastern shore of the Green River Reservoir in the former state park. Before his current project, Niklas had spent numerous weekends out here. He loved the lack of technology so much that he had bought the cabin a few years ago. Out here he was free—no fear of being watched or overheard.

He was standing at the shore gazing out on the almost glassy surface. *I forgot how beautiful it is.* He took a deep breath. It was a little chilly on that early spring day, but he wasn't expecting snow anymore. *One day I will live in a place like this. A lake, a cabin and nothing else around me.*

The sun was already setting behind him and this side of the lake was in shadow, but there was still light on the other side. He squinted his eyes. *Was there movement? They must be close.*

He turned back to the cabin to look after the stew on the stove. From outside, the cabin seemed like a lost and long-forgotten place. The years had gnawed the outside; the furniture needed another coat of color where the moss had not grown over it. Inside, the cabin seemed even more like it was from an earlier century. The sparse furniture consisted of a large wooden table with eight solid chairs, an old sofa, two rocking chairs and an old iron stove that spread cozy warmth around the cabin.

He barely had time to read a couple more pages of his book before the others arrived.

Jenny almost blundered into the cabin. "I'm glad you're already here and the cabin is warm. I'm freezing!"

Niklas grinned. "Didn't Eduard give you his pullover? That's not very gentlemanly."

"She already has it, and my jacket." Eduard entered the cabin right behind her, wearing only a T-shirt.

"It's beautiful out here," said Roberta when she came in. "Honestly, I didn't expect this. When you said 'former state park' I expected the worst: exploitation, overuse by tourists, like they did with the Bear Mountain State Park in New York and so many others. But this, this is beautiful."

"Nice to see you," said Niklas and gave her a hug. "You're right on time. The stew is done and the Malbec has breathed enough, so hurry and get to the table."

It took them a few minutes to get installed and gather round the table. The mood was jolly and they had a lot to talk about. August and Jenny were talking vivaciously about which courses she should take in college; Niklas observed with a smirk how August tried to nudge his daughter towards data and IT, she proved impervious against every attempt. Eduard continued to pepper Roberta with questions about writing and journalism, and she answered every one with laudable patience.

Niklas tilted his head. Roberta was too relaxed; she had not jumped at any reference to The Holding. *There's more to this visit. Something is brewing here.*

#

Niklas

The next morning Niklas and August got up at dawn to get wood to relight the fires in the fireplace and the stove. This was their routine when they were alone in the cabin and they didn't want to wake up the others. As they came out of the cabin, a breathtaking scene spread out in front of them. The sun had not risen yet, but it was already light and the hills on the other side of the reservoir were touched by early rays of sunlight. Mist lay like cotton right above the surface of the water, and hoar frost sugared the trees and the bushes around the lakeshore. It was perfectly silent, as if the whole world was holding its breath.

"Like a painting from Ted Turner in white." Roberta's voice came from the lakeshore.

They hadn't noticed her before and her remark woke them out of their marvelling. She had moved one of the outside chairs close to the lakeshore and lain on it, wrapped in a blanket. She must be able to see the whole lake.

"How long have you been out here?" asked August.

"Half an hour. I saw the last twinkling of the stars, how the sun painted a small, bright sickle on the horizon, and how the mist and the hoar frost created this winter's tale."

"It's unreal," said Niklas and they walked over to her.

Roberta looked back over the lake. Niklas couldn't see her face when she replied, but her voice had a sad undertone.

"I feel real for the first time in so long. I used to sit on my balcony in the city and watch people. I loved to travel, and by travel I mean discover new angles, meet new people, dance in Rio and get drunk in Dublin. I lost that. I lost the ability to dream."

Niklas didn't know what to say and, looking at August, he got the impression he must feel the same way. August's expression carried a sadness he had not seen in his friend before.

Roberta turned around and said, "It happened when I wasn't allowed to write what I wanted anymore. I hate my job." Her hands clamped around the armrest of the chair. "I'm writing the words of others. Worse, I'm writing the words of the system. I have to pre-publish every freaking article on a platform where tons of people can give feedback on it: politicians, PR managers, executives, or rather their assistants. I have to consider all corrections, regardless of if they're justified or not. It's as if I'm not entitled to have my own opinion. I die a little bit with every word. That's why I've quit my job."

"You quit your job?" asked Niklas, and in his surprise he felt a pinch of envy.

"Yes, I have. I plan to write a book. One about this dishonest world and the contemptuous way they treat human beings—the government, the big corporations, you name it—and about the return to serfdom in a country where you can only live if you have a loan and are not defaulting on payments. About the way this country is not worth surviving, and how it will not survive. Like the Roman Empire. There is enough power to oppress, but not enough willpower to solve problems."

August remained silent, but Niklas' thoughts were bouncing around. "It will collapse, and when it does, I will be prepared." He pointed to the cabin. "In there is all I need."

"I'm tired," said August with a flagging voice. "Tired of those people who only follow their own plans and think about their own wallets, even if they destroy the lives of millions. I could tell you stories that would make you believe we live in a dictatorship from the past century. Some ingenious, highly paid data scientist's only job is to design products and processes with one purpose: to exploit human weaknesses. There is an unofficial oral policy in The Holding's consumer loan companies to accept loans from defaulting clients and even increase them. That way, the chances are higher that the client will go bankrupt and we'll receive the money back from the Global Microfinance Fund."

"Isn't that fund meant to support microcredits in the Third World?" asked Roberta.

August snorted. "That's what you and the rest of America are supposed to believe. We support the weakest of the world by securing myriad microloans, while in fact we have legislation that allows companies to hand in US cases. Taxpayers fund it and The Holding drains 90% out again. It's a money-making machine. I'm tired of the system."

"One more reason not to trust those guys in DC, and the ones in Fairview even less," snarked Niklas.

August shook his head. "There are still things worth defending: democracy for example. Who protects that if I leave? It starts with me."

"And you want to do that alone?" Niklas looked down in front of him. *Leaving. What a waste. The rest of the world is the same anyway.*

"Maybe we *should* leave," said August after a while. "Olivia is fed up of it too. I didn't listen to her. I was too much into saying 'We would lose everything' or 'Who would pay for Jenny's college?' Perhaps..." He looked back out at the water. On the other side the white trees were colored by the first rays of sun.

"I'm happy you finally understand me. I almost lost hope."

They turned around. Niklas had not realized that Olivia was up as well and was standing in the door of the cabin.

"How long have you been standing there?" asked August.

"Long enough." Olivia tilted her head. "Since when have you had these thoughts?"

"A while—since I got onto the expert committee."

"Let's leave this country and start over somewhere else." Olivia came over to August and hugged him from behind. "We could get as much cash as possible without triggering an alert, sell the house and leave overnight."

"But where should we go?" August shrugged and looked at her. "It's everywhere here in the US. It's even in China—don't trust what people tell you on the street. And to go abroad we'd need to get our passports back from the loan insurance company. That will never happen with a sold house and frequent cash withdrawals. The moment we raise a red flag in the system that we're a flight risk, all our debts will default."

He's right, thought Niklas. *Once they have you, they won't let you go.*

"You never travel for business?" asked Roberta. "You could take your family with you and just stay there."

Olivia perked up. "That's it! You could visit that data center in the Alps and we could just stay there. You still have Swiss citizenship."

"The Holding would hunt us," August took a step back, "electronically and legally. I know too much about them. The Holding has strong ties with the Department of Defense and, so far, every country has bowed to the US. It's almost at the point that we'd need to fake our deaths and assume new identities."

Or kill the system, thought Niklas.

"I would be up for that too." Olivia's eyes sparkled with defiance.

A long, silent pause followed. Somewhere a bird got flushed out of the trees.

"Where will you go?" Niklas asked Roberta into the silence. "Writing a book of that magnitude in public would be suicidal. You would be labelled a member of an anarchy group, or even the Resistance."

The first rays of sunlight reached Roberta's face and she closed her eyes. "Why not give them a reason?" She looked back at them and her grey eyes got a dark, glowing shine. "I will go underground. I already have the contacts and they've prepared everything for me."

That's crazy. Niklas blew air through his nose and he saw August's eyes go wide and Olivia squint.

"But..." August started. He looked at Niklas as if he was expecting support in finding the right words, but Niklas was still sorting out his thoughts.

I've never met anybody who joined the Resistance.

"But that's like a death sentence." August's voice sounded scratchy. "You could never publish a news article again. With every purchase you would have to be afraid they would recognize you. Or even worse, they do and dupe you because they recognize you."

"I'll put up with it. I've been in worse situations around the globe." Roberta stood up. "I'll turn sixty this year and I haven't done half of what I wanted to do with the last twenty years. I became what I never wanted to become. Now is my last chance to

at least open some people's eyes. This country needs to change."
She shrugged. "What do I have to lose?"

I could help them. We should stay in contact, thought Niklas.

August stared helplessly at Roberta before he turned around
to Olivia. She was still standing behind him and only now could
Niklas see her face. She had her eyes half closed and her mouth
pressed into a thin line. Her cheek muscles jutted out as she
ground her teeth.

"What?" mouthed August, but she didn't even notice him.

Finally Niklas was able to grasp the straw of courage that was
dangling in front of his eyes. "I want to join the Resistance too,"
he said into the silence and everybody but Olivia looked at him. "I
hate the system as well, but I can be of greater help from inside. I
can get into IT systems, get information and change master data
without being detected." *With the back door I would fly completely below the radar.*

"That's laudable, Niklas, but I don't want to drag you into
this."

That was the point at which Olivia exploded. "How could
you?!" She took a quick step forward with her fists clenched.

The other three startled and took a step back. Roberta almost
tripped over the chair.

"You couldn't just go. You had to drag us into it, right!"

"I don't underst—"

"Of course you do." Olivia bared her teeth. "'I'm going underground and the last thing I'm going to do is spend a weekend with
my accomplices in the woods.'" Her voice shook. "But it wasn't
enough to have me and August suffer—you also had to destroy
Jenny's future. If I had known, I would have forbidden August to

even give that interview! What are we to you—collateral damage?"

"I didn't consider that, Olivia, I'm so—"

"—sorry?! You'd better be." Olivia's voice turned from volcano to icebox. "We're leaving."

August wasn't moving, and judging from his face he didn't know what to say, even less what to think. Roberta opened her mouth to say something.

"Shut up!" Olivia interrupted "You've already caused enough trouble."

"What's happening here?" asked Jenny. She and Eduard had come out of the cabin without being noticed by the others.

"Nothing. We're leaving. That's happening." Olivia stood there with her hands on her hips and her lips compressed into a line.

Jenny and Eduard still looked puzzled and Roberta had a facial expression that switched between defiance and sorrow.

"I'll join you," said Jenny into the silence and stepped down from the porch of the cabin.

Eduard remained on the porch, leaning against the beam with his arms crossed.

"Don't be stupid, girl." Roberta had found her voice again. "You have your whole life in front of you, and a boy with a great talent to write who loves you. Use this talent and try your luck, but don't go underground. You will be on the run for the rest of your lives."

Jenny turned to Eduard and tilted her head.

He pinched his lips after a moment. "I'm coming with you." He had stepped down from the porch and was now standing next to her with her arms crossed.

Olivia half turned towards Roberta. Her voice was as cold as before. "See what you've done. Thank you, Roberta, you just destroyed a family." She turned around and stomped towards the cabin. Briefly she stopped in front of the kids and yelled at them, "We'll talk later!"

It took a while for August to convince Jenny and Eduard, but eventually they followed Olivia into the cabin. Five minutes later they came out again and left. Olivia was steaming ahead, making sure that Jenny and Eduard were right behind her—they only peeked at Roberta and Niklas. August took two steps towards Niklas. "Whatever you do, please, just leave my kid out of this."

"I will. I promise."

August turned away, but a quick "Hey" from Niklas made him look back again.

"If you need a friend one day, you know where to find me," said Niklas.

August nodded and hurried to catch up with his family. Roberta and Niklas stood at the water and watched him rush away.

CHAPTER SIX

Fairview

August – October 22 – 2.5 Years to Day 0 (Burlington VT)

Anew reorganization, announced only three months after the trip, kept August busy. The Holding merged its supporting functions into one corporate center. The Supreme Court ruling in Miller v *The Poste* broke all the dams; both The Holding and The Corp could finally consolidate their power. It turned out that The Holding was double the size of The Corp, especially in IT.

'Welcome to the Future' was the slogan of the reorganization, but people on the floor just called it 'Company Tetris': same functions, just in a different order and with fewer employees. The big winner was Jude Dennings. He got appointed head of the new conglomerate within The Holding and with that he became responsible for the entire backbone; the Head of IT, Head of Marketing, the entire administration and even Legal and Compliance were now under him. Dennings was now managing more employees than lived in New York City and Los Angeles put together.

The reorganization also put a dent in Burlington. The city lost a lot of workplaces; the multiplex building was half empty and multiple houses in the Remules' neighborhood were abandoned.

August was glad they had artificial lawns otherwise it would have looked horrible within no time.

But August also made a leap forward. He was nominated Chief Information Officer of the entire Holding, directly reporting to Dennings, and as Head of IT August became responsible for over one million employees globally. At first Olivia had not wanted him to accept the nomination, but a throwback in their plans to start over had convinced her to go with it.

August had researched the rules of cash withdrawals and it had turned out that the net was woven more narrowly than expected. Selling their house without buying a new one would raise a flag and put more scrutiny on their transactions, so they had decided instead to max out their mortgage, withdraw small cash amounts and store them in a safe in the basement.

The safe was more Olivia's task, because from the moment August accepted Dennings' offer the reorganization filled his calendar 24/7.

Jenny and Eduard had started college in the meantime and Jenny saw her parents on long weekends only. Jenny and Eduard had selected universities in different states and saw each other even less.

One late evening in October, August came home late. It wasn't late in the evening, but he was late for a couple's dinner he and Olivia had agreed to do once a month to keep up at least some communication between them.

Excuses were going through his head while he trudged up the driveway. Every step felt like hard work and his jaw hurt. He opened the door and wanted to rattle off his excuse, but the hallway was dark, and so were the dining room and the kitchen.

The table was decorated and the pots with the now cold food were standing on it. A bottle of red wine was open and almost empty. August went over to his workplace in the library and poured a bourbon from the bar.

"You could at least offer me one as well," said Olivia from the door.

He swallowed the gulp he had in his mouth. "I'm sorry, I—"

"Never mind," interrupted Olivia. "I'm over that. It seems that we have to endure this until we have enough money to escape—assuming you stand still behind our plan. Just watch out that there's still a *we* when we finally get there."

August stood still without even trying to reply.

"You know what I did today? I checked out a cruise to the Caribbean, but I'm done now."

He took another sip from his bourbon. "Listen, I try to do everything right, but sometimes I just miss things or can't run out of the office."

"Sometimes?" Olivia laughed, but there was nothing hearty in it. "You missed half of Jenny's high school graduation, and while she was at her prom you spent the night in meetings with whoever."

August ducked. "But we both agreed—"

"We agreed? Don't get me even started! This all happened because you don't think. *You* had to invite Roberta over for dinner and on that trip. *You* had to report Gecko. Do you know how this is for me, waiting every day for somebody to knock on my door and ask questions about Roberta?"

"But nobody's come yet." August's arms dangled from his side.

"I don't care. If we had left when I proposed, we would not be sitting here and fighting."

August pouted. "That's not fair. I really try hard." He took another sip.

"It's not fair for me either," said Olivia in a suddenly calm voice.

Then she turned around and left. August poured another bourbon.

#

May 20, 2043 – 2 Years to Day 0

They didn't hear about or read anything from Roberta anymore and it seemed she had carried out her plans, but Niklas also seemed to have disappeared. August knew he was still around as he saw him online in the office chat, but he seemed to be avoiding him at any cost.

Even though August missed Jenny, Niklas' disappearance hit him worse. Niklas had been August's outlet and without this August swallowed his emotions. Sometimes he was tempted to tell Olivia about the wars in the office—Dennings seemed to love to 'divide and conquer'—but August couldn't drag her into this; it was enough that he had to endure it. Neither did he tell her about his aggressive daydreams or his anxious night dreams. He had to bear this, for the family. August kept his brain occupied and everything else submerged in his subconscious, until one late night, when August was on one of his usual night shifts working from home and Olivia was already in bed.

It was 1AM. August had the background of his VR goggles set to daylight so he wouldn't risk falling asleep. He was just about to send an angry message to the Head of Marketing, one of his peers, with a tired grin on his face—Dennings liked his angry messages—when he got an invite to a meeting the next evening in The Holding's headquarters in Fairview, Montana. August frowned. The invite was from Dennings and he pointed out that it was important that August appear in person. *That's less than twenty hours away. How the hell can I get a flight?* A pinching pain emerged behind August's eyes. He hit the send button on the angry message with his glove, took off the goggles and rubbed his eyes. Then he got up, walked over to the bar and grabbed a half-empty bottle of rum. He stopped in the middle of the movement. *No, not another one. She'd smell that*. He sighed. He went back to his desk and put the VR goggles back on to find a flight, only to give up again five minutes later. *Olivia will not be happy about this trip.*

#

May 21

Olivia wasn't happy when August told her about the meeting the next morning in the kitchen.

"You know that Jenny arrives tomorrow night and she'll only stay for five days?" She looked at August. "She was so looking forward seeing you this time. When did you see her last? Two months ago? Oh no, that's when you had an emergency workshop the entire weekend."

August looked away. "I know, but it will only be for one night."

"Don't get me wrong," Olivia sighed, "I don't mind you being away a couple of days. It pays our bills and brings us closer to our... plans. I just don't trust this Jude Dennings. You've aligned yourself with him, but that doesn't mean I have to."

"He's a slimy crook, but he is still my boss."

Olivia pressed her lips together and put her coffee mug into the sink. "I don't think you should go," she added after a moment.

"And how will I get away with that?" August felt a flare of annoyance boiling up. "Get sick? Tell him the flight was cancelled?"

"For example." She raised her eyebrows.

August shook his head. "Won't work. It's too obvious. He'll smell it."

Just as he finished the sentence, his Comm-Dongle rang. He got up and looked at the display. "It's him."

Olivia rolled her eyes.

"August," he answered the call.

"Jude here. Sorry for the disturbance."

"No worries." August turned away.

"I can imagine my meeting request last night must have created questions."

"Not at all, I'm just not sure if I can find a flight today, and I'm a bit under the weather."

"I understand, but it is crucial that you appear in person. We have strategic decisions to make. And don't worry about the flight—everything is arranged. A company jet will be ready for you at eleven and will bring you to Fairview."

"Eleven? That's great. I was worried." He shrugged and threw a help-seeking glance at Olivia.

"So we'll see you here tonight. And please say hello to your wife from me. I might be in Burlington later this year and I would love to finally meet her. It's a pity she missed last year's Christmas party."

"I'll tell her. She would be delighted."

"I would be delighted about what?" she asked after August had hung up.

"He plans to be in Burlington later this year and would love to meet you."

"Is that what he said? He would love to meet me?" She raised her eyebrows and sneered.

"Yes, and today seems to be a simple strategy meeting. See? It doesn't seem so bad."

"August, I love you for your good heart, but can you stop being this way when it's about your office? This just stinks—you never get called to headquarters. Didn't you tell me yourself that he likes you much more in Burlington, far away from the epicenter of power?" She narrowed her eyes. "He wants you to do something that's not right, maybe even dangerous, illegal or whatever. He can't even tell you on the communicator."

August opened his mouth to argue, but then he looked down at the palms of his hands and started speaking again with a much calmer voice. "I can't do anything about this. I have to go. You remember the victims of the big reorganization? We lost so many neighbors. Nobody lives here anymore and most of their homes are under foreclosure. I have to pretend that I'll play the game and put on a brave front, for us all."

"And jeopardize your whole family with it—for what? For nothing," Olivia threw at him. Her nostrils were flaring.

August shrugged helplessly. "I'd do that either way."

"Then use the time on the flight to think about what you want to tell Jenny—why you're away again when she's visiting us from college." Olivia turned away without another word.

Jenny. I should give her a quick call or send her a message. August knew Olivia well enough to leave her alone. She probably knew he was right, but she seemed to be too angry to admit it or too afraid of what might come. *I was right to not tell her the things from the office.*

August got up and made himself another coffee. Watching out of the kitchen window, he saw kids playing hide-and-seek in the abandoned neighboring houses. Where had he taken a wrong turn to end up in this?

Olivia wasn't upstairs when he went up to prepare his bags. He looked out of the window and saw her in the backyard, weeding.

She was still out there when he was about to leave, and unlike usual she didn't come over to the porch to say goodbye. He walked over to her. "I have to leave now."

She didn't bother to straighten up. "Bye."

"Bye, my dear. I'll call you when I arrive."

She continued to hack into the ground. August wasn't sure if he should wait or if that was it. After a moment he said bye one more time, turned around and left. As he drove out of the driveway he glanced into the backyard. Olivia had straightened up and she was looking in his direction. August couldn't see it, but he was sure she had tears in her eyes. He hated himself in that moment, but he had to go, for the family.

#

Fairview was artificial. August had never been here, but colleagues had told him that it was like a test-tube city. He had always thought that was because you only saw businessmen there, but when the jet circled above the city he realized it was the lack of suburbs that made it so unreal. Twenty years before, The Holding had left Seattle to benefit from a 100-year tax deal with Montana, and within a decade Fairview had grown from a sleepy nest to a city with a quarter of a million inhabitants and half a million hotel rooms. The social life was limited to the bars and theaters around the mall in the city center. Niklas had told August once that, as per one of those offshore news sites, after managers the second largest occupation in Fairview was escort services—despite the prostitution ban—followed by house cleaning.

August had taken business reading with him, but he could not work. Every time he had tried to concentrate, his mind had alternatively deviated to the fight with Olivia and the meeting ahead of him. He had felt queasy the whole flight, but now that the plane was approaching Fairview, anxiety grabbed him. *What could Dennings want? Why now? Have I missed something?* August bit on his lips until he smelled blood.

I won't be able to say no. My only chance is to catch the flaw in their logic. His thoughts were dashing around. *What do they want me for? To get rid of inconvenient employees? That would be too dangerous, even for Jude. But didn't he do exactly that with Gecko? Maybe leak something to destroy an enemy? It's a possibility, but why me? Does he want to send me away as well, like they did with Gecko? Did they find out about the trip to the cabin? Roberta.*

August started to sweat.

I have to find a way out!

#

(Fairview, MT)

August was still deep in thought when he left the arrivals building and headed towards the company limousines. He was torn out of his thoughts when he tried to get into the first car.

"That might be my car, unless you too are Ms. Jensen," said a lively female voice next to him. August looked up into a stunning smile; he saw little more than that.

"I'm sorry... didn't pay attention... Please... my apologies." He fumbled his briefcase.

"No worries."

And there was the smile again. August grabbed his carry-on bag and turned to the next limousine. He didn't want her to see him blushing, but he caught her looking through the rear window as she departed in her car, smiling.

It was a short ride to the hotel and the check-in was even shorter. For leading employees, everything was set up as if it was an office; even their iris scans worked. August also had a Fairview company credit card with a spending limit dependent on his rank—another specialty of Fairview. Every business in the city would accept this card and none of the details would leave the city limits. August got an executive suite, but he didn't pay it much attention. The tension had made him sleepy and he decided to take a nap.

When he woke up he didn't remember where he was at first. He was drenched in sweat and he was cold. Slowly the memories came back, of Fairview, the meeting, the fight with Olivia and the strange dream he had just had.

He had been driving in a car through Burlington. He knew all the streets, but somehow he was lost. It was foggy and after each corner the streets looked different than he expected. The street he lived on ended at the lakeshore, but when he reached the shore the street made a curve and he drove through the coffee shop at the Lakeshore Plaza. People did not seem to care when he hit the tables with his car.

He drove for hours like that and then his wife was sitting next to him. He didn't recall her being there before and she insisted that he should drive on the left side of the street as they were in New England. August was glad they were alone on the streets otherwise they'd probably have caused an accident. A car passed them and pushed them from the street. They overturned and landed in a ditch, but miraculously they were not hurt. August jumped out of the wreck and shouted in the direction of the disappearing car that he hated him. Then he started walking home. He was alone again, and when the car came back he knew it wanted to kill him. He started running, but the car came closer and closer until August was able to recognize the driver. It was himself. That was the moment he woke up.

Checking his Comm-Dongle, he realized that he had slept for almost an hour and that his wife had called twice in the meantime. He dropped back on the bed and closed his eyes for a moment before he called her.

"Yes?" Her voice still had an undertone, but August wasn't able to categorize it yet.

"Hey, honey, sorry I didn't call. I guess I'm just too nervous about the meeting."

"I know. Were you sleeping when I called?"

"Yeah, took a nap."

She paused for a moment. "I wanted to wish you good luck with the meeting."

"Thank you."

"I also wanted to remind you that you are not alone."

"I know."

"That's good."

"I have to go."

"Sure."

"Bye, honey."

"Bye."

After they hung up, August frowned. Had that been an encouragement or a reprimand? 'You are not alone' could go both ways, especially the way she had said it. August shook his head and went with the encouraging version. He took a shower and afterwards he felt a little better. He still had about three hours left until the meeting would start, but he didn't know anybody here. Dennings had done a great job of keeping August out of headquarters. For a moment he sat at the corporate desk in his suite without a plan. He decided to go the hotel bar and watch the businessmen come and go.

The lobby was busy. August sat down on one of the sofas placed randomly in the hall, ordered a strong coffee and gazed at the hustle and bustle. *Funny,* he thought, it's like ants in a farm. *Well, sometimes it feels like that. So, who's the queen in our ant colony?* August chuckled.

Every now and then, between all the drones in suits, he spotted a woman in a business suit, but still Fairview was a man's world. He picked faces and tried to imagine the stories behind them, but most of the ones he came up with were very similar: man with a family at home, living a kind of a double life, loving and responsible at home but reckless and ruthless at work. Another one had a wife at home and a mistress here in Fairview, and last but not least there were the DINKYs: no idea why they were still together, going for luxury vacations twice a year and only seeing each other for breakfast, if at all, because each of them had their own program.

August thought about Jenny. He wished he had reached her to tell her he would be on a business trip, but she had not picked up, so he had left her a message and promised to make up for it. *If only she and Eduard could live the lives they want to and evade being pressed into a mold or cubicle.*

"Did you finally find a cab?" asked a voice he recognized but wasn't able to assign to a face. He turned around, recognized the smile again and blushed. *The woman from the airport.*

"Yeah, it was next in line, I hope." August staggered to his feet and tried to smile away that awkward feeling.

The woman smiled too and his brain went blank again for a second.

She turned her head away and looked at the line in front of the bell desk.

"It's funny watching them chase their small distractions, knowing the vast majority miss out on what's important," she said with a more reflective expression.

August had a moment to look at her: blonde hair, a slight snub nose and a typical business uniform—suit, heels, white blouse—but with a red bandana around her neck that gave her a bold expression. And then there was that smile, like when the sun comes out after a storm.

"We're supposed to be drones in a way, right?"

She turned around and smiled again. "Drones—that was the word I was looking for. By the way, I'm Adriana, a data-scientist drone."

August noticed a light Southern accent in the way she pronounced her name.

"August Remules, CIO."

Adriana gasped. "Jesus, I didn't recognize you. I'm sorry... I didn't mean to..."

"No worries, first I'm human, then American, and then somewhere in there CIO."

"I have to go... an appointment," she said and stood up.

He could see a light blush on her face before she turned around and scurried away. The crowd of men in the lobby divided as she walked through them.

August spent another hour in the lobby observing the drones, and several times he caught himself scanning for a red bandana in the crowd. Then the guy at the bell desk gave him a sign that the limousine had arrived, and only minutes later August was sitting in another large but this time empty lobby, waiting to be called into the meeting. The man at the service desk had asked if he wanted a coffee or a drink, but August had declined. He knew Jude would offer him one too, and he wouldn't accept a no. The company logo behind the desk was so massive that it almost appeared menacing.

#

Niklas – (Burlington, VT)

Niklas was shivering in his IT bunker. He had hated night shifts before, but since they had switched off the servers, the temperatures were freezing down here. The heater beneath his desk helped a little, but only for his legs.

With the switch to the new data centers, the servers were not necessary anymore, and they had switched them off. Now they were standing in front of him, half in the dark, dead and menacing. The technicians had not been moved as they had hoped, but laid off. Niklas didn't miss them, especially not David; the air felt fresher without him. They were only three database specialists left, and Niklas' job had gotten boring. The small issues were fixed by an operations team and there were just not enough big issues to fill his day—and there were only so many interesting things on the web.

"User logged out," said a cheery female voice that tore Niklas out of his trance of randomly clicking through the internet. He checked his watch: midnight. *Right on time*. He chuckled. Niklas had created a bot that tested the back door every five minutes and it ran on autopilot. Whoever wanted him to create this back-door entry must be high up in The Holding's food chain to keep this a secret. *If they knew that I know about this, they would get rid of me,* he thought. *That's probably the reason they got rid of Michal; they think he did it on his own.* He chuckled again, but it turned into another shiver.

The back-door entry had been used every night between 10PM and midnight, like a Swiss watch. *For whatever purpose— who would know anyway? There's a reason it's called 'untraced'.* He clenched his clammy fingers and with this movement a thought sneaked into his mind.

I could use the back-door entry to create my own back-door entry.

A feverish bustle grabbed him. He took off the VR glasses and gloves and got up. He rushed to the men's room and afterwards to the pantry to get a coffee. His thoughts were jumping back and forth, and when he got back to his desk ten minutes later he had a plan.

Niklas shivered with excitement when he put the VR glasses and the gloves back on. He logged in using the back-door entry and started working. Two hours later he had created his own back-door entry, and added direct satellite access to the moon data center and an audit log that would log all changes executed with the two back doors, hidden in the moon data center. *This will be my insurance policy, hidden and still accessible every night.* He would just need a satellite antenna. "Whatever you do now, I'll be watching you," he said out loud.

He checked the time. Still over two hours until the others would come in. *I need a cover-up. The moment they find irregularities they will hunt the source down,* he thought and got back to work. Within an hour he had created a complete fake identity, including a history back to his date of birth. He had figured it was best to stay close to reality—less risk of accidentally give his real identity away when he was using the fake one. He leaned back and crossed his arms. *Welcome to the world, Rick Sandberg.*

CHAPTER SEVEN

The Proposal

August – 2 Years to Day 0 (Fairview, MT)

From the lobby, the elevator brought August up to the top floor. The main building was seventy-five stories and had the shape of a triangle, resembling a sail. The other buildings around it were smaller: forty stories in close proximity and twenty in the next row.

When August got out he stepped immediately into Dennings' office, although 'office' didn't sound like the right word. It was more like a hall: fifty feet wide, eighty long and two floors high. It was dimly lit, but slowly August's eyes got used to the light and he noticed further details. The main entrance was on the far side and August realized that he must have been let in through a side entrance. The large conference table with virtual meeting equipment to his right, and the bulky mahogany desk in front of the large windows on his left appeared lost in the room. On the opposite side of the room an Art Deco spiral staircase led to a gallery. August couldn't gauge how deep the gallery was, but he saw light shimmering from the back. He seemed to be alone. There was no screen on Jude's desk; maybe he followed the New Age top management work style to lead without technology. *No, not Dennings*.

August straightened his tie, walked over to the window and was blown away by the view. He could see half of the city from up here and he was sure that during the day he would have a great view of the plains from up here.

"On a clear day I can see the Rockies."

August turned around and saw Dennings standing in a small doorway beneath the spiral staircase. He walked towards August and shook his hand.

"I would love to see that." August noticed once again the out-of-phase smile.

"You will like this feature as well." Jude took his glove and swooshed his hand from his desk to the window, which turned into a gigantic transparent screen. On the bottom of the window the streets were named and little icons showed the location of restaurants and stores—even people were tagged with their names and organizational codes. The named highways and routes exiting the city looked like beams of light, and in the distance dotted lines indicated the peaks of the Rocky Mountains. Above everything, the window showed the stars and the constellations. A light green dot marked 'AA1387' moving from the east towards them, and another one seemed to descend towards the Fairview airport.

"Amazing." That was the only word August could utter for several minutes.

"Wait until later tonight when we turn to the other side."

August flicked his head slightly back.

"This floor rotates twice every twelve hours. You can feel it a little if you concentrate. I hope you don't get sick like I did at first. I didn't eat for almost a week."

"Sometimes I look over the woods from my office in Burlington, but this is amazing." August could only shake his head.

"Let's go upstairs. It's more comfortable there. We have a lot to discuss."

The dimensions of the gallery surprised August when they arrived upstairs. It had the form of a giant mushroom that was cut open in the middle at the stem; where August was standing right now it was about fifteen feet wide, but it turned into a round room with a diameter of thirty feet and a circular sofa in the middle. The robot bar to August's right gave out cold light, but other than that the room was even duller than the rest of Jude's office. There were already people sitting on the sofa, each with a glass in their hand—familiar faces, but August couldn't place them. The dull light and the smoke from the cigars blurred August's view, but it hit him like a hammer hitting a nail when he got closer and recognized them.

"Gentlemen," said Jude when they arrived at the sofa. "May I present to you August Remules. He's my most valuable manager." Jude turned to August. "Henry E. Mitchell, leader of the Republican Party in the Senate, and Anthony Lang, leader of the Democrats in the Congress. And you know Daniel Harrison, head of our PR Department."

August swallowed hard. What is this? What are they doing here? The smoke was scratching in his throat. "Senator Mitchell, Representative Lang, it's an honor to meet you."

"That's way too formal for this hour and that aged bourbon. Henry and Tony." Senator Mitchell pointed at himself and Representative Lang before he stood up to shake August's hand.

Are they part of the meeting? August felt heat welling up and he started to sweat underneath the suit.

After they had all shaken hands, they sat down again. August had barely sat down when he was poured a glass of bourbon as well.

"Well, August, how is Vermont these days?" asked Senator Mitchell.

"It's nice. Still a little chilly at night, but it's getting to be summer soon. The first real winter in years was a godsend for the remaining ski resorts."

"Other than tourism and The Holding, there isn't much business, right?" Representative Lang chuckled. "Well, there isn't a lot of business outside The Holding across America."

Jude shrugged. "Don't forget The Corp."

"Right." Lang continued, chuckling.

"There's still a large part of the population in the farming and agriculture industries. We're always competing against Wisconsin with cheese and the rest of New England and Canada with maple."

August's answer was ignored.

"Aren't you from New England too, Daniel?" said Jude.

The Holding's PR manager had just been listening so far, but now he adjusted his horn-rims and opened his mouth.

"Anyways," interjected Senator Mitchell before Daniel could answer, "shouldn't you be more communicative as PR manager?"

"You would be surprised how much good listening does in PR." Daniel put on a sleek smile. "But to answer your question, I'm from Maine, although I haven't seen it much since I left for college. Studied political science at George W. Bush College in Anchorage."

August raised his eyebrows. "I always wanted to meet somebody to tell me first-hand how it is."

"It's a great college with an even greater faculty. Our most important leaders teach—they know politics from their own experience."

"My son was there," said Representative Lang, "and Henry's kids too."

Jude stood up and walked to the bar. He was eating something when he returned and August realized that he hadn't eaten since the lunch on the plane. Hard alcohol on an empty stomach wasn't a good idea.

"Have an appetizer, August." Jude must have noticed his glance. "We'll have more food coming later."

August also went to the bar and had some of the sophisticated finger food. He stayed away from the mini crawfish; they seemed to watch him. When he came back with two horse-meat sliders, he noticed that they had poured him another bourbon.

"Founding the Anchorage college was the best idea we could have had," Senator Mitchell picked up the conversation again, "and it was absolutely necessary to bridge the gap between the two parties."

"Only that way have we been able to get rid of the fundamentalists. Damn Tea Party was no better than the socialists," added Representative Lang with a grin.

"I always thought Anchorage was an initiative from the Tea Party to streamline their members." The bourbon was loosening up August's tongue.

"That was part of the master plan. The GOP financed it—"

"—together with a lot of funding from the Democrats," interrupted Representative Lang. "Within three years the university board was fundamentalist-free and it's been a success story since then, thanks to Jude and The Holding's big data capabilities. We truly live in a post-fact era."

I can't believe what I'm hearing here, August thought. *These are trusted leaders and they're almost bragging about this.*

A buzz interrupted them.

"That will be the food," said Jude and they moved downstairs to the conference table, which had been turned into a banqueting table. They stuck to small talk during dinner, and by the time they went up to the gallery again they left three empty bottles of Malbec behind.

"What are your children doing, Henry?" asked August.

"You mean do they have real jobs, or are they in politics too?" Henry chuckled at his own joke. "Let's see. How many children do I have? Seven in total. Three are in politics, two in finance and two married to politicians."

"The Kennedys, the Bushes and the Mitchells," said Tony. Now everybody was smirking.

In the little silence that followed, Jude rose to speak.

"You might be wondering, my dear August, why we summoned you tonight. Let me first give you a wider view on the matter. Soon the United States of America will celebrate its 275th anniversary—a respectful age, and what have we accomplished in this time? We have risen from being a handful of colonists to the greatest power in the world. More Nobel Prize winners live in this nation than in all the other countries put together. We shaped this world, not only with our power and inventive talent, but also with our understanding of democracy and our efforts to perfect the system. We were and always are a step ahead. Look around you; most developed countries have a two-party system now. This is the foundation of an elite democracy, the highest form of government. In Anchorage we train new talents to do their duty for their country from federal to town level. There, away from all the disturbance, they can discuss the future of our nation. It is a beautiful system, but it needs a centerpiece, somebody to ground the elite and tie it to the people, and the people need a leader they can follow—one from of their midst. Somebody who has been successful in life and achieved great things."

August got a feeling of foreboding, and with every word the whole situation became more and more surreal. It was as if he could take a step back and watch himself sitting there with the others, each of them with a glass of bourbon in one hand and a cigar in the other. Everything started to turn. He couldn't hear what Jude was saying anymore, but he could hear his blood rushing. Seconds seemed to stretch into minutes and minutes to hours, until the words came clear and crisp out of Jude's mouth.

"And that is why we want you to be our next president of the United States of America."

In the following two eternal seconds August felt all eyes on him. *What? No!* He jumped to his feet as best as he was still able to and lurched towards the door behind him, which he assumed was the bathroom. It was, but August didn't care at that moment.

He bent his head over the toilet bowl and threw up like he had not done since his 21st birthday. He felt better afterwards, until he remembered the message he had just received and had to vomit again. Then he flushed out his mouth to get rid of the bitter bile and looked into the mirror. What he saw shocked him to the core. His eyes were sunken and red from alcohol and smoke. *No way I'll do this. We would never be able to leave.* His skin was yellowish and his hair tousled. *We'll be squashed between our debt, the scrutiny of the process and the office, always on the edge of losing everything. What if they find out about the trip to the cabin with Roberta?* August's heart made a jump. He took some deep breaths and washed his face, but the pale yellow color wouldn't go away.

"Everything all right, my friend?" asked Jude, knocking on the door.

"I'll be back in a minute," said August with a voice that didn't seem to be his. *Olivia will never agree to this.*

He washed his face again without changing the outcome, took a deep breath and went back in. The smoke itched his eyes. Jude was standing next to the door and the others were still sitting on the couch, grinning at him like college freshmen at their first party. The smoke got into August's nose and the sickness came back.

Just don't give them another laugh. August sat down again.

"I feel honored by your proposal," he said. Slowly his logical thinking returned. "Unfortunately, I can't become president." A thought flashed through his mind. "I wasn't born in the US." *That's it, the loophole.* He chuckled. *They didn't think of that simple thing.*

"That won't be a problem as of next week. We can't change the Constitution, but it is a little hazy there. The law to clarify that is already in place," said Tony.

August let his shoulders drop. His brain was playing pinball. *I need to gain time.* "Which party should I run for?" August looked into Jude's vain smile and realized this was the wrong question.

"The Republicans," said Tony and pointed to Henry. "We're not yet there with gaining a majority, but we will be back in the Oval Office in eight years."

"You will be our quarterback for the next eight years, and what we've seen so far excels what Jude promised us." Henry patted August on the back. "You are the perfect man. I have all the formalities with me. You can join the party within the next few days, and after a short trip to DC to meet some people, we will be ready to position you as a candidate."

August glanced at the empty glass in his hand. *When did I drink this?* In the corner of his eye he noticed Jude sitting up. Everything smelled like a trap. The alcohol and the smoke were wiped away and terror grabbed him. *No, no, no, no.* August could hear his heart beating through his temples. He stood up.

"I need another drink," he murmured.

Jude stood up as well and followed him to the bar. "Another bourbon or maybe a gin? We also have Cuban rum from before the end of the embargo. Try one."

While Jude poured the rum, his face came closer to August. "Actually, I don't want to lose you, but you wouldn't be doing this for me—it is for your country."

August didn't reply; he looked at the glass of rum in front of him.

"And don't worry about your current job." Dennings continued talking without even expecting an answer. "We've found a successor and he's already accepted. You could begin working out your campaign immediately."

August looked up and wanted to say, "You can't take away my job, I played all your stupid games, I deserved it," but Dennings' insistent eyes stopped him.

Jude tilted his head. "And I have put a great deal into you. My name is in this too."

There was one thought that emerged more and more out of the cloud of a million thoughts: how could he escape this? *I have to put on a brave face and sabotage it later.* His thoughts got lighter again. *That shouldn't be difficult; a scandal here and there and I would not even survive the primaries.* August put on the best smile he was capable of and reached out his hand to Jude. "Agreed, I am your man."

Jude put on his vain smile again. "That's great!" He shook August's hand and patted his shoulder.

They turned towards the others and Jude announced, "Gentlemen, we have our next president."

They applauded.

"August, we appreciate your support and dedication." Jude clapped his hands together. "Let's clarify the rest tomorrow morning. Let's say 10AM. I think we're all tired."

On the way out, Jude held August back. "We have a lot to do. I think it's best you tell your family that you have to stay a few more days. My assistant will arrange the necessary with your hotel."

Jude's voice seemed to be very distant. August nodded constantly. *Out. I need to get fresh air.*

"Also, it goes without saying that everything we discussed today has to be treated with the greatest confidentiality, even towards your family for the time being."

Minutes later August was sitting again in the limousine on his way to his hotel.

#

May 22

The cold, clear night tore August out of his numbness. The limousine had dropped him in front of the hotel and now he was standing there, forlorn and shivering, wavering about what he should do now. He was tired and restless at the same time. Going to bed now would mean tomorrow would be right around the corner, and he wanted it to be as far away as possible.

"Can I help you, sir?" A hotel employee approached August.

"Where is the closest monorail station?"

"Right here behind the hotel. You can go through the lobby and turn right at bar."

"Is there also a way around?"

"Through the garage, sir."

"Thank you," said August and turned away, but out of the corner of his eye he saw the man's Adam's apple moving and guessed he was talking into a neck microphone. *He's informing Dennings.*

As soon as August was around the corner, he hid in a dark spot to watch the employee. He did nothing suspicious, so August left after a moment. While he was waiting for the monorail, he wanted to call Olivia, but he wasn't ready to burden her. *Not yet.*

Five minutes later the train arrived and August boarded the last car. It was almost empty, just two businessmen sitting in a row, discussing some market performance. One of them looked up and eyeballed August.

August frowned, looked away and looked back; the guy wasn't looking anymore. August sat in a seat three rows behind them and two stations later they got off. He didn't have a plan of where he wanted to go; he needed to empty his head. At a station that looked like there was entertainment down a side street, he got off too.

The side street turned out to be a fake main street with a saloon, an English pub and a few differently themed bars. August selected the one with the loudest music. It was a James Bond retro-style bar. The light was dull and he needed a moment before his eyes got used to it. It was more a lounge than a bar and it reached over three floors. The ground floor was a complete circle with a hole in the middle from where August could look down to the other levels. The lowest level had a dance floor which was pretty filled. One level up a lounge area followed the circular shape and it almost seemed that the only purpose of it was to watch people on the dance floor. The bar on the ground floor also followed the circular shape of the room. August took the last empty seat at the bar and ordered a beer. The disco beat and the general noise made it hard to grasp a single word or sentence. He looked around, but he didn't recognize anybody. He took out his Comm-Dongle and played with the idea of texting Olivia, but that would mean opening a discussion which he wanted to avoid tonight. He wished nobody but Niklas was here. August selected

Niklas' number and then remembered that calls out of Fairview were monitored. He let his shoulders drop and put his Comm-Dongle away.

"Your beer, sir. Paid for by the lady over there."

"Excuse me?" August turned his head so he could hear the barkeeper better.

"Your beer was paid for by the lady over there." The barkeeper made a sign with his head towards a woman standing a quarter of the circle further down. August didn't recognize her. The light in the bar was set up in such a way that you could recognize what was next to you, but the further away you looked, the dimmer the light became. The barkeeper leaned closer and added with a lower voice, "I have to warn you, sir. Despite the prostitution ban, there are still pros in here from time to time."

"Thanks." August took his beer and moved towards the woman. He felt his heart beat faster and at the same time a red light went on in his head. As he got closer he recognized the smile. His heart jumped and his mouth got dry. He couldn't resist taking a gulp from his beer.

"Thank you for the beer," he said when he got close enough. She made an inquiring face and he repeated it louder and raised his glass. She picked up her cocktail from the counter.

"I had to make up for my clumsiness this afternoon."

It was hard to understand her; August was more guessing than hearing. She added something, but it was too difficult to make out. He tilted his head. She leaned forward and he automatically leaned forward as well. She repeated into his ear, "A beer? In this city of cocktails and champagne?"

Her perfume got into his nose. "I needed something honest."

His joke lit up her smile and he caught himself trying to think of another joke to see the smile again.

She leaned forward again. "I'm sorry for this afternoon."

"No worries, I had an acute loss of memory. Hi, my name is August Remules from Vermont. Nice to meet you here. Are you new in town?" He winked.

Now she had to laugh. It was less bright then her smile but very much worth the sound.

"I'm Adriana Jensen from Alabama. Pleasure to meet you too."

August looked around a little. After a moment he asked, "Are you on a business trip or do you live here?"

"Usually I work in the Mobile office in Alabama, but my boss had some important meeting and needed me for a special tasks. I'm kind of his SWAT team."

"I would love to have such a SWAT team."

She smiled.

"Another one? I'll buy this time." August looked at her empty glass.

"Sure. It was a Troublemaker."

It was cramped at the bar and August had to squeeze in to order. He felt her leg pressing against his and when he turned his head a little her face was so close he could have easily kissed her. She just looked him in the eyes with hers wide open. He felt an erection coming and tried to turn his hip so she wouldn't sense it.

While August was stretching himself a little to get noticed by the barkeeper, she was jostled in the back and fell into him. He couldn't help but catch her. His face was now so close to hers he smelled the sweetness of her drink in her breath. *Now she must feel it*. When he looked down into her face, she had her mouth a little open and her eyes lowered. After an eternal second she stepped back and said, "Sorry." He couldn't hear it, but he saw it on her lips. The barkeeper noticed him and walked towards them.

She leaned forwards and lit up her smile. "It's too crowded in here and too loud to have a decent conversation. Why don't we go somewhere... calmer?"

Heat welled up in his head. August nodded with a time delay. One minute later they were out in the cold again, walking down the little street.

"It's hard to find somewhere calm," said August after they had passed a German beer place and a tequila bar. He had to make a great effort to resist the urge to hold her hand or lay his arm around her shoulder. He didn't recognize himself, but he pushed the thought away.

"True blue. Why don't we have a drink at the hotel bar? I mean, we're both staying at the same hotel."

"Makes sense." August couldn't say any more—he was concentrating too hard on keeping his distance without losing the closeness while they walked.

"But let's get a cab. I don't want to wait for the monorail."

As they walked towards the main street she linked arms with him and leaned on him.

"It never gets this cold in Mobile," she said, shivering.

Now he dared to lay his arm around her and he was almost disappointed that there was already a cab waiting on the corner.

"I bet the bar will be empty." August looked at his watch. It was already past midnight.

When they arrived at the hotel the bar was closed.

"That's too bad. I would have loved to continue our chat." She pursed her lips.

"I have an executive suite." It took August a moment to say the words. "I could order a bottle of champagne."

She raised her head just enough to look into his eyes. She opened her mouth to say something, but then she bit her lip and just nodded. They rushed to the elevator and down the corridor to his room.

#

The sex was not good. She came—twice, he thought—but August didn't care. For him it was about discharging anger and frustration. With that gone, he felt left alone with the weight of the world.

"That was a hurricane," she said into the silence and added when August didn't react right away, "I hope you liked it too?"

"Yeah, it was great."

"Something wrong? I thought we connected."

"It was great." He leaned up on one elbow. "But now, lying here, I feel helpless against all these important decisions and the pressure that comes with them. And I can't tell anybody." August didn't know what drove him. He needed to talk and there was nobody left to talk to; he might as well talk to a complete stranger.

"I understand, your job demands a lot. Don't you have anybody you can talk to?"

She made a sign towards his wedding band. August hadn't even bothered to take it off. He shook his head without saying a word.

"I can be a good listener and I have a terrible memory," she said with an earnest smile.

He looked at her for a short moment and then he started talking, slowly at first, and leaving confidential points out, but with her understanding all the dams broke. He told her about the invitation late at night and the fight with his wife, the meeting and the indecent proposal; the word 'indecent' only came after a short breather, but yes, it was indecent, ethically reprehensible and simply disgusting.

"That is a special offer." She frowned for a second and looked him in the eyes. "I would at least consider it. Imagine the things you could do as president. Ok, you'll spend eight years in a golden cage, but you would never have to work again. And you could change something. You have no idea how I would love to be able to change something in the world."

August said nothing, but she must have read the 'but' on his face.

"What are you worried about?" She lit up her smile and crawled over to August. "If your wife doesn't want to, I would move into the White House with you."

August tried not to hear that last part, but it crept into his brain. *Yeah, that would solve my problem.*

"I would be selling myself. That's what bothers me most."

She frowned again and sat up. "We're past that. All of us do that, simply by playing our roles in the system. We sell our free will the moment we take on debt and start living our lives on credit cards. Whoever doesn't can't play anymore and falls back with no hope to return. You know about the large trailer cities with thousands and thousands of trailers, don't you? You already sold yourself. This offer is your paycheck. Question is, do you have the guts to cash it in?"

Her brisk, innocent courage forced his lips to smile. "Perhaps you're right. I could use a consultant like you when I'm in the Oval Office."

She laughed and lay back in August's arms. "I would need a hazard bonus. Your wife would hunt me."

August didn't reply. He tried to push all thoughts away, but the harder he tried the faster the carousel turned in his head. As the pictures fused, the whole world became clear to August: he had two choices, no more, no less. He could become president, sell his pride, maybe lose his wife, or he could get ejected out of the system, lose everything and drag his family down with him. *Both choices are wrong. I just have to select the least wrong one.*

August was torn out of his thoughts when Adriana stood up.

"I have to get up early today. Sorry about that. I would have loved to stay the whole night." She dressed scantily, gave him a long kiss, lit up her smile at the door and was gone before August could even think an intelligent thought. He stood up, poured himself a Scotch from the hotel bar and went back to bed, but he fell asleep before he even nipped at it.

#

The ringtone of August's Comm-Dongle woke him up. He needed a second to get his senses together, and when he did a horrible headache kicked in. *Olivia.* He closed his eyes and picked up the communicator with shivering hands. *What do I say?*

"Good lord, finally! Why didn't you call? Can you imagine how worried I was?"

"Um, I'm... sorry. It was a long meeting and, you know, I thought you were asleep..." August swallowed to get the itch out of his throat. Swallowing hurt his head.

"Right, and texting is so outdated."

"I'm sorry, really."

"*Jaja*. You're so focused on your job and yourself, you don't even think somebody else could be worried. And I know about your meeting, I can hear the drinks and the cigars in your voice."

"It's not my fault. I can't be the odd one out." He hated the whiny tone of his voice, but he couldn't help it. "But I was responsible," he added quickly.

Olivia paused for a second. "So what was it that he didn't want to tell you over the phone?"

"I can't tell you yet, but it's not something bad per se. It's still highly confidential."

"You can't or you won't? I'm your wife, for Christ's sake. Whatever it is, it affects me as well."

"I can't... not over the communicator. And I have to stay for a few more days to finalize everything."

August heard her grasping for words.

"You know what? Marry your job and go to bed with it."

Beep. She hung up.

August let himself fall back on the bed. He tried to remember last night, but his headache only let him see fragments. He didn't remember how they had got back to the hotel or how they had ended up in bed, but he remembered the bar, the sex and the talk afterwards. *I have to be at Dennings' office by ten o'clock,* he thought after checking his watch. If he got up now he could grab a strong coffee before he had to be there.

#

August managed to be on time, but when he entered the building a bit of bile came up. It was just a little gulp, but it was enough to make him remember all of last night's meeting. At 10AM sharp he was let into Dennings' office. Dennings was waiting in front of his desk, looking towards the other door. August looked as well and saw a blonde woman leaving the room. She turned around and smiled at August before closing the door.

Adriana? His heart jumped off a cliff.

"Who was that?" August tried to ask offhandedly, but he heard his own voice trembling.

"You should know her. Adriana is Chief of Staff. I heard you met her at the bar yesterday," said Jude casually.

August's ears felt as if they were glowing and his pulse was pounding in his neck.

Jude continued in his casual tone. "My dear August, how could you? We were lucky you told her and not anybody else. You haven't, right?"

"No, no, I haven't... I didn't want to... It just happened... I didn't think..."

Jude gazed at August and the bile taste in August's mouth became overwhelming.

Then Dennings nodded. "No worries, it can happen. Your wife doesn't need to know." He took a step towards August and patted him on the back, but when August heard the word 'wife' he winced.

"But the violation of secrecy is a serious matter."

Dennings took a step back and his eyes held a mixture of sternness and worry.

"This could be the end of your career. Under normal circumstances, your discharge would be being discussed as we speak." He came closer again. "August, we need somebody we can absolutely rely on. Somebody with an outstanding track record for integrity. You have to understand, we are offering you the most powerful position in the world. I need to know if you are our man—no backtracking, no excuses and no loopholes."

August was still looking down.

"Are you our man?"

A hushed "Yes" was the only thing August could utter.

"August?"

August looked up and Dennings looked him in the eyes until August averted his gaze.

Dennings signalled August to take a seat. "Well then, let's start. We have a lot to do. The others will arrive in half an hour and we'll start by sketching your profile and your campaign. Adriana will be your personal assistant for the campaign and your two terms. Her duties will also involve keeping in contact with our group here. You understand, August, that we won't be able to meet after you're announced. August, are you with me?"

August nodded, but the only thing he had heard was "Adriana... personal assistant..."

"Have you already told your wife—"

August flinched.

"—that you'll have to stay a few more days?"

"She wasn't too happy about it. I might need to call again later today."

"I thought something like this might happen. That is why I called her right before you arrived. It appears more credible and strengthens your position. Moreover, we can prevent your little slip-up from causing problems in your campaign. I also told her you won't be able to call her as you are under tremendous pressure, but she shouldn't worry. If there is anything urgent, she could call my office. I calmed her down a little and she wants you to know that she understands."

"Thank you." August couldn't say any more, but he was grateful. While he had been worried when he arrived in Fairview, now he was scared. Scared to lose everything he cherished. Everything he wanted to protect.

Dennings continued to talk, but August had stopped listening. He had reached a point where everything was lost, and that feeling didn't let him go. The rest of the day passed like a film: the meeting with the leaders of the two parties, the definition of his profile, the sketch of his campaign. Only his official introduction to Adriana remained in his memory. He almost couldn't shake her hand. A part of him hated her and another part wanted to hug her and cry. That second part denied that they had tricked him and hoped for a sign from her that she was sorry and she meant it seriously.

It was this moment that remained with August when he was sitting in his hotel room in the evening. Armed with three ring binders—no online data for security reasons—about his new profile, and a fourth one about the campaign, he had been escorted by company security back to his room. It was then that an untold rage had grabbed him—about Adriana, Dennings, his wife, everything. The more he thought about it the bigger his wrath became. He threw the folders into a corner and stood there with his fists clenched, looking around at what else he could maltreat. He grabbed his e-pad and threw it against the wall and when it didn't break he picked it up again and dashed it on the wooden floor. The floor got damaged, but the e-pad not so much. He took the chair and smashed it onto the e-pad, once, then a second, third and fourth time until he eventually threw it against the hotel room window. Nothing seemed to break, which increased his rage even more. After another five minutes he had tilted over the desk and the bed.

In his rage he had not noticed the three security guards who had entered the room. They could barely overpower him before he threw the TV screen against the wall.

As he lay there on the ground, held down by three guards and only wearing his shorts and socks, he realized that he had been broken. With that thought he let his body go limp, and as if that wasn't mortifying enough he soiled himself for the first time in almost forty years. Disgusted, the guards let go.

"He's done, Frank," said one of them and a guy with a bulky head approached him.

"We'll wait outside. Clean yourself up and then we'll get you a new room. And *behave*. You don't want Mr. Dennings to hear about this."

August didn't need to look up to recognize the guy. His sneering tone was enough; it was the guard who had been there when he met Dennings for the first time. *Frank. Right, that was his name.*

They left the room and August Remules, CIO of The Holding, married, one child, forty-nine years old, next president of the United States of America, remained alone in his room.

CHAPTER EIGHT

The Resistance

Olivia – (Burlington, VT)

Olivia was still frantic about the phone call she had had with August half an hour earlier. She had already had a bad night, with a mix of anger, worry, guilt and heartburn, but August's stonewalling and the collusion made her even more furious.

She was restlessly cleaning random stuff—books, ornaments, the kitchen floor—completely out of her mind, when a video call came through via the home communicator. The caller ID was blocked. Olivia frowned. After the new counter-terrorism laws had passed ten years earlier there were only a few people and organizations left who were allowed to withhold their caller ID. Olivia hesitated a second before she pressed the 'I'm coming' button. She took a short glance in the mirror to straighten her hair and took the call.

"Good morning, Ms. Remules, how are you?"

"Mr. Dennings, I... I'm fine. I didn't expect your call. I just talked to my husband."

"That's why I'm calling you. I assume it was an unsatisfactory call as he isn't allowed to share any details."

"I'm used to that." Olivia's comment came out brisker than she wanted, but then again, she couldn't care less.

Dennings frowned so briefly she almost missed it. "I am sorry about that. It's part of the position and the regulations that come with it. We are preparing very important strategic decisions and your husband's contribution is indispensable. He probably won't be able to communicate with you over the next few days. We are all under great pressure here. I'm sure you will understand it as soon as he's able to tell you. However, as a small thank you I have granted him five vacation days next week and taken the liberty of arranging for a trip to a luxury resort in the Caribbean for the two of you. I hope that compensates for the inconveniences."

Olivia had not interrupted his monologue a second time, but now he seemed to expect a reply. She forced a smile. "That's great!"

Jude frowned again, this time visibly.

That was a little too much, I guess, thought Olivia. "Thank you very much for this. Does my husband already know?"

"Thank you for your understanding. It is great to see that August has somebody at home who supports him. That is worth a lot."

Does August know? He never actually answered that question.

They both said goodbye. Olivia gaped at the blank screen when Jenny's voice startled her.

"A week in the Caribbean, that's nice."

Olivia turned around and looked at her daughter. "Yeah, that *is* nice—too nice. I can't get rid of the feeling that something is wrong, and this Caribbean trip fuels it even more."

"What could be wrong? Is Dad in trouble?"

"Your dad sounded as if they wanted something questionable from him. They've singled him out and put pressure on him." Olivia pressed her lips together and looked out of the window.

"Maybe they want him to announce huge lay-offs or communicate a security breach. Dad would really mind that."

"That would not have this level of secrecy. And it can't be illegal. Dennings said that your dad will be allowed to tell me. No, it's something that will affect us and I'm afraid they will reach their goal to lure him in. You know your dad: if they threaten him with taking away our nice life or your education, he would sacrifice his life."

Jenny eyes gained a worried shadow.

Olivia stood up and took her in her arms. "Don't worry, darling. There's nothing we can't solve if we stick together as a family."

She felt Jenny nod again in her arms.

"Do you want something for lunch?" she asked to guide her and Jenny's moods to another topic. The ache in her stomach had gotten a little better and perhaps eating something wouldn't be a bad idea. "You could tell me a little more about college. Is Eduard also in town? I bet he is," Olivia added with wink.

That comment made Jenny smile again.

"You know me too well," she said, following her mom into the kitchen.

"That's my job. I am your mom."

"He'll be over later this afternoon. He promised to help me with a paper and later we're heading over to friends'."

Olivia opened the fridge and got out a couple of containers of leftovers: some vegetable stew, artificial chicken meat and a large one with mac and cheese. "That's nice of him. What's the paper about?"

"Nothing dramatic. A comparison of the political systems of different countries. They want me to put them on a timeline showing the evolution and, obviously, they want me to show our system as the most evolved."

"They said that? I wonder why they would tell you how the results should look."

"No, they didn't, but it's the professor's opinion and everything else is wrong."

"That doesn't sound like a good course." Olivia put two pans on the stove and threw the leftovers in.

"Maybe I should stir it up a little," Jenny said, more to herself. "I could draw a different line and argue that the latest might not be the best. Or I could make a tree and put them at the same stage, showing that they are just different categories of the same kind."

"I'm not sure if that's a good idea, Jenny. I understand that the paper is meaningless, but I don't think you should risk anything for something so unimportant. It's not good for your grades and you don't want to end up on a list, do you? That could be the end of... you know what I mean." Olivia tilted her head and looked at Jenny.

Jenny pulled a face. "I wouldn't be surprised if I'm on a list already."

Olivia felt the tension in her stomach again. "What have you done?"

"Nothing, Mom, don't worry."

"So why would you end up on a list?"

"I told you that I'm in that debate club, and Eduard is too in his university."

"Yes, what about it?"

"There are alumni that went underground—"

"You have to get out of there immediately!" Olivia's heartburn was back.

"But why?"

"Why? Because you don't want to ruin your future! Why didn't you tell me?"

"Oh Mom, I was just joking about the list. It's not a big deal. There are thousands in that club all over the country. Anyways, I would be surprised if they knew."

Olivia looked at her daughter for a long moment, pressing her lips together as if she wanted to prevent herself from saying something. Then she sighed through her nose.

"Just be careful. Promise me."

"I am. Really. I promise."

#

Jenny

Jenny didn't know how long the awkward silence lasted afterwards. The only audible sound was the sizzling of the mac and cheese and the chicken in the pan. She was glad it was interrupted after ten minutes by the AI. Or maybe it had only been two minutes.

"One person at the front door."

"That must be Edu," she said. "Camera, front door on screen."

Eduard's bright smile appeared on the screen.

"Alarm off and unlock front door," Jenny said on her way to the front door.

"Unlocked."

Eduard could barely close the door behind him before Jenny jumped at him. They kissed as if they had not seen each other for a year rather than only two months.

When they got back into the kitchen her mom had put three plates, each filled with leftovers, on the kitchen island.

"Hi, Eduard. I guess you want some as well?"

"Hi, Ms. Remules."

Jenny's mom tilted her head and wiggled it a little. "For the tenth time, I'm Olivia."

"I tend to forget." Eduard smirked.

Jenny poked him. "Don't be such a wisecrack."

Jenny and Eduard sat down on the bar chairs next to the kitchen island and looked at the mountain of food on their plates. Jenny's mom remained standing and started eating.

"How are you and how is college?" asked her mom.

"It's great. Well, almost." He smiled at Jenny. "If only it wasn't so far away from Jenny."

"I heard you're even in the same debate club—"

"Mom. Don't start again, please," interrupted Jenny.

Eduard looked a little puzzled. "Did I miss something?"

"Mom's scared we're too rogue in our debate club."

"I didn't say 'rogue'. I just meant—you know exactly what I meant."

"Olivia, I can assure you we are careful." Eduard put on an even more sincere face than usual. "We know it doesn't take a lot to be misunderstood and that you can't get rid of a label once you've got it."

Her mom let her shoulders drop. "I'm sorry, there's just too much going on at the moment. I don't want you to think I don't trust you."

Jenny and Eduard shook their heads and Jenny opened her mouth to say something, but her mother continued before she could start.

"Your dad and I didn't want to drag you into this while you were away, but you know we always keep everything open at home." Her mom picked at her food without eating. Only sporadically looking at them, she told them the political games and trench warfare August had had to go through over the past year, the long nights spent worrying where the next attack could come from. After she had finished they felt disheartened. Eduard looked down.

"Your dad didn't tell me any of this. He tried to protect me, but it's hard not to overhear those late night conversations. And he gets easily annoyed. I see how it nags at him," her mom added and bit her lips.

Jenny needed to say something, but the best thing that came to her mind was, "Mom, it's like you said: we'll get through everything if we stick together."

"Yes, I did and it's true," she said and tried to smile but didn't succeed. She took a rapid bite of her food. "But I don't want to hold you up. Didn't you come over to help Jenny with a paper?"

"Yes, he did," Jenny said. "Let's go upstairs."

"Take some mac with you." Olivia gave them each a plate and they left.

After they closed the door behind them, Eduard took Jenny in his arms and they stood for a while.

"Are you hungry?" he asked.

She shook her head. "It's just Mom's way to get over something."

"Shouldn't we have told her?" he asked after a moment.

Jenny shook her head. "She's worried enough. Something's wrong in Fairview. I wish I was a mouse so I could sneak in." She hated Dennings for what he was doing to her dad.

Eduard sat down on the bed. "Do you think she's right? I mean, about us risking our future? Ending up on a list?"

"These rumors about lists have been spread to create fear, and fear helps the establishment to control the masses. What are we doing? Sitting in a room or around an old two-way radio and exchanging opinions. What could be wrong about that?"

"We are taking it a level further now."

"Don't be such a wimp," Jenny said with a provocative grin and poked Eduard.

He didn't bite. "I'm not a wimp. I'm just saying we should be thoughtful."

She pouted. "Look, the Resistance is not violent. It's our civic duty. They do nothing more than discuss the current situation and do campaigns to get media coverage. I... we would never go into a violent splinter group. You know that."

Eduard kept silent, but the look in his eyes showed Jenny that he wasn't convinced.

"See, they always threaten people by saying they'll lose every-thing. Look at my parents—they're scared to death to lose all this. They say it's because of my education, while in reality it's more about losing what they think they've achieved. You heard my mom—my dad twists and buckles every day. What would be so bad about living outside? Yes, it would mean less comfort and less luxury, but it would also mean less pressure and lies."

"I know, but there's always a risk." He tried to shrug.

"Yes, there is. But if society doesn't want to have responsible people that want to discuss how this country can improve, I don't know if I want to be part of such a society." She smiled and hugged him. "You will see tonight. These are nice people. I' sure."

#

That same evening Jenny and Eduard went to the address the Resistance cell at her college had given to Jenny. It wasn't far from Jenny's parents' house, but with every turn the houses appeared more run-down, even worse than the abandoned houses in their neighborhood; some just desperately needed to be paint-ed, but others were a veritable dumping ground.

Eduard was awfully quiet the whole way. Jenny felt a little nervous, but excitement took over the closer they got. It was the same mix of sensations she knew from when she was a kid and she would sneak out of the house to watch the stars from the lakeshore. She was worried Eduard would draw back at the last minute.

Although it had gotten dark in the meantime and the streets looked more menacing without lights, they parked the car a cou-ple of streets away and walked the rest. When they turned into the street with the right house, he stopped.

"Do you think we're doing the right thing?"

"Everything else will be worse for us if we don't."

"You're probably right," he drawled. "I've thought a lot about us and our future, and we have to do it for our kids too. How could we stand in front of them later and explain why we didn't even try?"

Jenny gave Eduard a hug and then they walked hand in hand to the house down the street. A sign in front of the house stated, 'No trespassing—violators will be shot'. Jenny hesitated to open the gate and looked up. From what she could see without a streetlight, this house was one of those that needed painting, and shingles were dangling from the roof. The vegetable garden, however, was in perfect shape.

They were expected. An older man opened the door and waved them in without password, explanation or identification. Eduard signalled Jenny to be cautious. *Does he smell a trap?* Jenny looked around, but she couldn't make out anything specific in the dark entryway.

The man peeped outside through the blinds. After a minute he turned around and made a sign for them to come with him. Without a word they followed him to the basement. Now even Jenny was alert. In the middle of the stairs they passed a kind of bug scanner; a small green light blinked and the man grunted, satisfied. Down in the basement they followed a small hallway to a door. Dim light from inside the room shone under the door. Jenny wondered what would happen and who had a basement nowadays anyway?

The man opened the door and, inside, four people were sitting in a circle under a dim light cone; three chairs were still empty. The rest of the room was pitch dark. It was hard to recognize anything, or any faces, but the tension fell off Jenny when she moved closer to the light.

"You're in too?" she exclaimed and gave Niklas a hug.

"Of course. I'm glad you're here," he said and whispered into her ear, "I'm Rick Sandberg here. Tell Eduard." He continued in a normal voice, "We need as many as possible," and then whispered again, "I would have talked to you earlier. I realized you had so many questions, but I promised your dad I wouldn't."

"Dad knows you're... here?" Jenny raised her eyebrows.

"No, he doesn't. He just asked me not to drag you into this, but now you're here on your own."

"And we're glad as well, right Eduard?" Jenny looked over.

Eduard had kept himself in the background, but now he nodded carefully.

"May I introduce myself?" interrupted the man who had let them in. "I'm Jacob. I'm chairing our little group here. I also founded it twenty years ago. I'm happy our campus group led you to us. We have a lot to talk about. Please, take a seat."

They both sat down on the two empty chairs. Despite her excitement, Jenny still noticed suspicion in Eduard's eyes.

"Before we start with the usual agenda items, I would like to welcome two new members, Jenny and Eduard. They are both from Burlington. However, as they are both studying outside the state, they will only participate in meetings or campaigns from time to time." Jacob took a small pause and looked around with the expression of the mayor of a village. "I suggest we all introduce ourselves. As I already said, I am Jacob. We only address each other by first name," he added towards Jenny and Eduard.

"Before my retirement I was working as a carpenter in the union until I lost my job at fifty. They accused me of being a member of the Resistance. Ironically enough it was that event that led me to join." He chuckled. "Anyways, I was lucky never to trust the banks. I kept most of my savings at home and so I can live off them. Sometimes I still do carpentry jobs or help out in a bar."

After he had finished, he looked around and flicked his head to the young woman to his right.

"My name is Hanna. I am his granddaughter. My parents are both politicians and this keeping up a clean facade makes me sick." She acknowledged her statement with a sassy nod.

Jacob looked down when Hanna was talking as if listening to her upset him.

"I grew up in a world of lies and pretending that everything was perfect, had to be perfect," Hanna continued. "At the same time I saw this poverty and injustice. Human beings abandoned by civilization along the way. However, my ultimate decision to become active in the Resistance was based on what happened to Grandpa. We founded this cell and found like-minded people— like you."

The people in the circle nodded. The girl next to Hanna continued. Jenny estimated her to be only a little older than herself, but when she stared talking she appeared much younger.

"I was the last one to join—well, before you now. My dad doesn't know I'm part of the Resistance." She put on a clandestine look. "My life was boring, so I changed something. But I also wanted to make a difference. My fiancé excludes people from loans and each evening when he comes home he tells me how many he has killed today as if he's proud of it. I kept it to myself for a long time, until I met Jacob at a bar. I drank a little too much and told him everything. That's how I joined the group. Oh yeah, and my name is Lauren."

She looked at Niklas.

"Well, it seems it's my turn, although you should already know everything about me. My name is Rick. I work at the centralized Holding IT and I joined one and half years ago. As a database specialist I always have a lot of insights into the system and at one point I decided to do something against the unfairness."

"That was also my reason," threw in the guy next to Niklas. "My name is Martin and I also decided to do something against the system, but I don't think we're doing enough. We should take action to hurt the system. Something that draws attention to our cause. What we do is piffling trifles—"

"We already talked about that, Martin," interrupted Jacob. "We do nothing that hurts people or damages anything. The real Resistance follows the traditions of Martin Luther King and Gandhi. Civil disobedience and non-violence are our mottos."

"But we achieve nothing with that."

"Enough. You don't want to scare our new friends away, do you?" Jacob gave Martin a chiding glance and then he turned to Jenny and Eduard. "We do not take part in any militant activities. We are convinced that change can only come peacefully."

They both nodded hesitantly.

"Pacifism is very important to us too. Violence only causes more violence," Jenny said and clasped Eduard's hand.

"However, freedom of speech is a cornerstone of our movement," Jacob added mildly. "In here everyone is entitled to their own opinion and so we can have different opinions and even arguments, but we never lose our common goal: non-violence is the only way to true peace."

Jenny and Eduard nodded again, this time without hesitating. Jacob seemed to be satisfied and he turned back to the whole group.

"Let's get rolling. We have important points on the agenda." Jacob started by sharing two recent developments from their sister cells: a successful flyer campaign in Seattle and something about secretly reducing the cash withdrawal amount for surveillance purposes. Afterwards, each gave an update about something they were working on—apparently a flyer campaign in Burlington.

At the end, only Niklas had not said anything. Jacob looked at him.

"Rick, anything from your side? You always have special projects."

Niklas sat up. "Unfortunately I'm very busy at work at the moment and can't spend too much time on planning. But let me give you a quick overview of where I am. I found a way to get IP addresses without blowing our cover. If we took the IP addresses of subscribers to the *Business Review*, we would have 70% percentage coverage of the top and middle management of The Holding and other companies. I can hack the list on the internet without leaving traces behind."

"You're a database specialist—couldn't you just download the list?" Martin leaned back in his chair and shrugged aggressively.

Niklas sighed. "That would give away my identity."

"Why do you need those IP addresses?" asked Eduard.

"We don't, but another cell has asked us if we have that kind of information."

"How many cells are there?" asked Jenny, raising her eyebrows.

"We don't know," said Jacob. "We only have contact with two other cells and when I say 'we' I mean four of us—one main contact and one deputy for each sister cell. The whole Resistance is only loosely organized. No cell knows more than two sister cells, not even the Leader."

"The Leader?"

"The Leader is the head of Cell Number One. Nobody knows him, except the two contacts and their deputies. We get our orders from one of our sister cells and communicate them further to another one."

Jenny looked down and peeked over at Eduard. They'd discussed at length how the Resistance might be organized. Eduard had always thought that there must be some kind of central council elected by all the members. Jenny had disagreed as the transparency would cause an increased risk of detection, but even she hadn't thought it was this loosely organized.

Eduard didn't seem to be satisfied with this answer. He squinted at Jacob. "But how do you know the questions or orders don't get altered along the way?"

Jacob put on a mild smile. "We all want the same thing. You would know if an order or question did not convey that notion."

Eduard looked down and curled his lips. Jenny could tell he was not satisfied at all by this answer.

"Anyways," said Niklas into the silence, "I can have the list ready next week and give it to you, Hanna, for the other Burlington cell."

"Thank you, Rick, for the risk you're taking," said Jacob. "You mentioned something else, something big."

Niklas didn't answer right away. "I'm working on that major project." He stopped for a second as if he felt a little uneasy. "It seems The Holding is building a revolutionary data management and storage system, where all data is mirrored between three locations on different continents and a fourth one on the moon. And when I say 'all data' I mean *all*, including third-party data of clients, social security, FBI, Department of Justice, American Airlines, Bank of America and many more. At the same time, the data has to be available anytime, anywhere."

Isn't that the same system mom was telling dad about two years ago? thought Jenny.

"I don't understand, Niklas," said Eduard. "This is a simple concentration of storage centers and it's a known fact that The Holding stores 80% of America's data and a little less globally. Where's the revolutionary angle?"

"There will be no back-ups anymore."

Eduard blew out air through his nose. "But that's insane! One hacker attack or virus and the data is gone." He shook his head.

"That's the reason the system has to be airtight. It has to resist power blackouts and virus attacks. Look, conceptually the system is brilliant. The four databases are hosting basically the same data. Changes are done to all four simultaneously and are logged separately. If there are inconsistencies, three databases beat the fourth one and two equal entries are investigated in a dedicated quality management department. The system even works when one database is down. It is simply ingenious."

"So if it's so ingenious, where is the angle for an attack?" Martin sneered, annoyed.

"If you manage to change the data in three different locations simultaneously, it is regarded as true forever. As I said, the architects are so convinced that their new system is unsinkable, they've waived having a back-up system. It's this arrogance that's their Achilles' heel. I planted a program code in the update and in the mirroring sequence which allows me to change entries in the four databases at the same time. And then I programmed the log code so that updates from a specific robot user are not logged. Since two days I have a way to change any data without being seen or detected. We could alter the names of people who are suspected to be in the Resistance. We can create fake identities to protect us. Martin, I could make you rich. I could make you president of the United States, for Christ's sake."

Niklas smirked around the circle. Nobody dared to talk and even their breathing seemed to be too loud.

"But wouldn't that be detected?" Eduard said. "I mean, we're not yet in 1984."

"You're right. As soon as they realize, they will shut me out and check the data against the old back-ups. But there are other opportunities. We can either change only small things that will help our cause, such as getting rid of someone's debt or deleting an amber or a red flag, or we could wait five or ten years and create a major disturbance in the whole system. By then, the old back-ups would have no value anymore."

Martin jumped up. "Why wait? We should attack at the first opportunity." His eyes were fiery.

"These are very interesting thoughts, but they don't help us here and now." Jacob's resolute intervention startled Jenny. "We have to be very careful how we use this. The chances that this means liberty are much lower than the risk that it could get worse. It could be the end of the Resistance, or we could end up in another civil war, or even worse, finally drift into a dictatorship."

"It has to get worse before it gets better. Evolution takes far too long," said Martin with an alarmingly calm voice.

He clearly wanted to say more, but Jacob quickly started talking again. "This is too big for us to decide now, but as we heard from Rick, we still have time to develop a master plan. I propose he goes quiet until it is ready. We'll exclude him from our meetings going forward and he'll come back as soon as a plan seems executable. I'll nominate the contact person later. At the same time I'd ask the connectors to inform our sister cells in 31 and 42 days that in about five years we will have a weapon at hand that will allow us to change the game without shedding blood."

The others nodded; only Martin kept his arms crossed. Jenny observed his struggle to fight down his anger with a mixture of amusement and discomfort. "That's all rubbish anyway. You know what I believe: you're just trying to be important," she heard him say to Niklas in a low voice. Niklas ignored his comment.

In the meantime, Jacob wrapped up the meeting and the participants left one by one at irregular intervals.

Lauren was first. Before Niklas left, Jacob took him to the side. "Be mindful what you do, Rick. Great power comes with great responsibility. We don't want to become what we fight."

Jacob lowered his voice and Jenny couldn't hear more. Niklas nodded and shook Jacob's hand firmly. Then he waved to Jenny and Eduard and left.

After about half an hour it was Jenny and Eduard's turn to go and it seemed that Jacob wanted to keep Martin behind to have a serious talk. Jenny and Eduard left the house, turned right and walked down the street like a couple in love, which they were.

CHAPTER NINE

Friendship in the Dark

Olivia – May 28 – 2 Years to Day 0 (Burlington, VT)

Olivia was just coming in from the back of the house when August came home. She heard him enter the front door, say hello and go upstairs without an additional word.

"Everything ok, honey?" she called when she reached the bottom of the stairs. No reaction; she just heard the clicking of the master bedroom door being closed. *What's wrong with him?* Her stomach was churning. She rooted herself to the spot and looked up the stairs for several minutes before she shook her head and went into the kitchen.

Maybe he needs time. But still, he's never behaved like that before. He had always at least said something like, "Let's talk later." Her grandmother used to have an old proverb from her home country: a jar goes to the well till it breaks. *I hope they did not break him,* she thought and worry started to gnaw at her.

She kept herself busy cleaning the kitchen, but when he had not come down two hours later the worry began to pester her to the point that she had a hard time breathing. Olivia was glad Jen-

155

ny had gone back to college. It saved her from having to come up with another shallow excuse for her dad's behavior.

That night Olivia had to sleep on the sofa. Despite asking and even begging, he had not unlocked the master bedroom. The cracking of the wooden floor told her he was walking around. She was restless and could only sleep when it was almost dawn. August woke her up only half an hour later and he looked as if he had not slept either. His sunken eyes were matt and the pupils tiny.

He sat down in the chair opposite the coffee table. "They want me to run for president," he said without looking at her.

Olivia sat up. "Of what? The Holding?"

"No, the US. And I accepted." He looked like a heap of misery. "I couldn't fight it. They made me say yes. I couldn't..."

"That's... that's..." Olivia closed her mouth again. "I don't know what to say," she began again after her mind had tried a dozen other sentences. She crossed her arms. "I don't like it. Not at all. But looking at you I see you don't want it either." Olivia felt her fast, superficial breath.

August looked up. "I don't."

He stood up and slumped onto the sofa next to her, but even though they had sat like this a million times before, it was different this time. There was a wall between them.

Is it me or is it him?

August got up again and walked towards the kitchen. He turned around in the doorway, opened his mouth and closed it again. Olivia knew he wanted to ask her if she wanted a coffee too, but somehow the question seemed to be awkward.

"If you can't do anything against it, we will stand behind you," Olivia heard herself saying.

He pulled a grimace. "I can't oppose it openly. I have no idea what would happen if I did. My old job is gone anyways. All I can do is hope not to get elected."

"If that's the case, what happens if you don't get elected?" Her fists were clenched beneath her crossed arms and the fingernails were hurting her palms.

August said nothing. He just stood there and looked at her.

He didn't say anything for the rest of the day and not much more in the months after. Sometimes he would lock himself in the library for hours. The campaign wouldn't start for another year, he had explained to her. There would be charity events and speeches; some of them she would be expected to take part in, but most of them he would do alone. He wouldn't bother her with more than was necessary. Time passed, but the wall remained. It got even worse. They started fighting. Not that they hadn't fought before, but now the fights were unrelenting and there was no reconciliation afterwards. At first it was about news of him or how to get through this together; later it was about how Olivia taunted him that he was spending more time with the coordinator of his campaign—that blonde bitch—than with her, but more and more it was about small things until it was about everything.

"You do what you have to do," became Olivia's standard phrase.

#

August – March 28, 2044 – 13 Months to Day 0 (Fairview, MT)

The increasing tension between August and Olivia had not gone unnoticed in Fairview. Shortly before the start of the actual campaign, August was called to Fairview once more. He was surprised as Jude had made it clear they wouldn't meet anymore. Maybe Adriana had contrived this—she had her own mind anyway and despite what Olivia thought August had hardly seen Adriana in the preparation of the campaign. Most of the time she called into the meetings from somewhere and it almost seemed that she was being pressured to not give away her location. The rest was just left to the campaign team. He wondered what her agenda was in this.

August sensed that something was wrong when he stood in front of Dennings' office door. Usually the security guard would hold the door, but this time he didn't move an inch.

Maybe they cancelled the campaign. Desperation can create cruel insinuations. A jolt went through August's body, just to get a dark touch again. *What would happen then? I'd lose everything.*

It took some strength to open the door. He had never realized how heavy it was. Dennings was sitting behind his desk and looking at an e-pad. He only looked up, looked to the chair in front of his desk and then continued to look at the e-pad. The chair looked tiny in front of the desk and the desk only got larger when August came closer. The sun screen was turned off and winter sun drowned the area around the desk in bright light. He sat down and waited. Dennings didn't show any sign of attention.

August watched every move carefully. *I've done everything they wanted. What's wrong? I sold them my soul.* August gaped at Dennings' face, trying to get a glimpse of what was wrong.

Dennings didn't look up, not even once. After ten minutes Dennings' assistant appeared, bringing him a cup of tea. August expected to be asked for coffee, but even he ignored him. August's mind tried to escape the tension, but every time it reached its goal, Dennings made a small move—a sip from his tea or a frown—that brought it back. Within minutes, the glaring sunlight hurt August's eyes.

"We need to talk," said Dennings finally without looking up.

August could only swallow.

"I have to admit that I am in fact a little disappointed in you."

Now he looked up and his eyes pinched August. August's face froze.

"You promised to do everything to support your campaign and yet you are sabotaging it."

"I... I don't understand." Waves of hot and cold wafted through August's body.

"What were you thinking the weekend before last, not bringing your wife to the charity event? We were counting on you."

August crooked himself into the chair. "I am really sorry, but she didn't feel well."

Dennings shrugged and sighed. "I would understand that if it had been the first time. However, since we started our project you haven't been seen a handful of times with her in public—and no, paparazzi photos don't count."

Dennings had stood up while he was talking and walked around the table without taking his eyes off August.

"It's still difficult for her to be so present in public." August cowered in the chair and for a moment he was scared Dennings would hit him.

"See this photo here—" Dennings showed him what he was looking at on the e-pad. It showed August and Olivia one month ago at a reception; August was walking ahead and Olivia was two steps behind with a stony face.

"Not exactly a happy couple, right? And here—" Dennings showed him another photo. "You were clearly fighting. You look like a coward. Nobody wants to have a coward as president. Hell, nobody wants a coward as an employee." He walked to the large window and looked out.

Again the sunlight glared at August. He wanted to say something, but he didn't know what. Twice it crossed his mind to say he'd better quit, but he had the gut feeling that was what Dennings expected, and August didn't want to imagine what reaction Dennings had planned for that. What did he want?

"I really tried, but I will try more."

Dennings didn't turn around. "I remember very well the day you left here. You promised us you would talk to your wife and she would support you."

"I can't change her. You have to understand that she has her own will." The chair became even more uncomfortable than before and August sensed his foot falling asleep.

As if this was his prompt, Dennings sighed again and slowly turned around. "Then there is only one solution to this. You have to go your separate ways."

It took August a moment before he could articulate anything. "Separate ways? I don't understand."

"I am a simple guy. If it doesn't work with your wife, we will need a divorce. But I can promise you that your family will be taken care of. Money will not be an issue—"

"Never!" August jumped up. His leg gave in and he had to support himself on the table. His heart was pounding in his temples. For a moment he thought he would pass out.

Dennings looked down and carefully shook his head. "But will this work?" he said softly. "We both know, the way it's going now, your campaign is doomed to fail. So why bother at all and spend the money and effort?"

This is not true. He can't ask for this. He can't. August had to breathe heavily, but he still felt as if he couldn't get enough air. "If you expect this, you'd better look for a new man."

Dennings looked up. "I'm not your enemy, August. I am on your side." He maintained strong eye contact. "Over the past couple of years I've been protecting you and your family. You know that, right?"

August didn't answer, but inside he sneered. *Protecting us? From what? No way would he do that. Anyway, what would be worth fighting for without my family?*

"I had to pull some strings so that your daughter wasn't taken in for conspiracy. You knew she was meeting with the Resistance at her college, right?"

August wasn't sure what he felt anymore.

"Looking at your face, you didn't." Dennings tilted his head. "Also, your wife hoards cash in your basement. Don't worry about the anti-money laundering red alerts—I took care of them. None of your loans will default, but I couldn't help wondering what she needs that cash for." Again that careful shaking of his head. "Anyway, you see I am on your side. However, it took me much more effort to prevent your little slip-up *here* from going public. Somehow a journalist must have heard about the affair and started digging. But I'm not sure if I can protect you any further."

August didn't want to listen anymore. He turned around and scampered out. He heard Dennings say that he'd be out for three days but they'd catch up later in the week. Neither the assistant nor the guard tried to hold him back.

August hoped that the cold air outside would wake him up. It didn't. The entire world seemed like he was seeing it through cotton wool.

They were expecting him at the hotel. "You shouldn't stay outside for long without your winter coat. Luckily they brought it over from the office. Next time you'd better call a limousine."

August didn't listen and went straight up to his room.

After closing the door behind him, he stood in the middle of the room without knowing what to do. His brain went blank. For minutes he wasn't even able to think of what he could do until he finally grasped a thought. *I need a drink.* He looked at his watch: 2PM. *The hell with this. The hell with all these conventions. The hell.* He turned around and walked straight out of the room, down to the lobby and out through the main entrance. Just outside, security held him back.

"Let me call you a limousine, sir."

"I'm good." August hesitated, but then he saw the other guards blocking the driveway and he realized that he would not be free to leave. August let his shoulders drop and nodded.

He let the driver drop him off downtown at the street with the bars. He went straight into the nearest one—a western saloon-themed location—and ordered a beer.

"We have only light beer in the afternoon, sir," said the barkeeper after he had swiped August's Fairview company credit card.

August grimaced, turned around and left. After he heard the same sentence from the third barkeeper at the third bar, followed by "company policy", August sighed and sat down. He looked around and realized that he was in the same bar where he had met Adriana a little over a year ago. The place was half empty, or half full depending on what you would expect for the afternoon. August caught himself looking around for Adriana. He shook the thought off. *Why would she be in this bar at this time, or in Fairview, anyway?*

Two hours and four beers later he had convinced himself that she might actually show up, but he was still surprised when she appeared in front of him shortly afterwards.

"I thought you might be around here when they told me at the hotel you left in a cab," she answered the question in his eyes. "You missed our meeting."

"Hi, nice to see you too. What meeting?"

"I sent you an invite as soon as I heard you were in town, about three hours ago. You haven't checked your Comm-Dongle, I guess."

"No more meetings today. I'm done."

August looked at her. She looked back. *Something's different. The smile. She hasn't smiled yet.*

Adriana frowned slightly and looked at his beer. "Light beer? I am surprised."

"It seems they only have this in the afternoon." *Was there something like a smile? Just a little one.*

"A lager, please," she said to the barkeeper and turned back to August.

There it was again, the smile. August relaxed.

"That's one of the funny little secrets of headquarter city you only get to know when you live here," said Adriana with a wink. "Every visitor has an alcohol quantity limit. It depends on your rank, the importance of your visit, your meeting schedule, etc."

"I've got a set diet?" August wasn't even surprised about this.

"You probably have the status 'Important/Social' so you can drink but you should still be able to get up in the morning. Be happy they didn't set you on 'Social/Crucial' or 'Business only'."

"You live here now? No Mobile anymore? You didn't tell me."

"I still have my place down there, but I figured it was better to live up here, tax-wise. I bought an apartment about half a year ago."

The bar was getting crowded.

"Let's go someplace locals go," said Adriana out of the blue.

He looked up. "Locals?"

"They let you pay cash when you appear local. Legally they would have to check, but they know me at some places."

August nodded and he left his light beer half done.

At first, the cab driver they found at the corner outside didn't want to drive them to the street Adriana told him. She had to show him her letters with her local address. He grunted and let them in, but for half the ride they had to endure his sermon about how dangerous it would be if he had not insisted on proof and that he could lose his license if he was found out.

Adriana rolled her eyes and smiled at August. She swiftly touched his leg with her hand. "You look troubled. We should have a real beer and you can tell me what's on your mind."

"A real beer..." August looked out of the window. Dozens and dozens of uniform houses passed by outside. "I'm just not sure if I can cope with what's expected of me."

"Let's talk there." Adriana flicked her head towards the camera in the front.

The bar was located in the town center of old Fairview and was like a relic from the past century. It was dark inside, except for the spotlights at the bar and over the pool table. The smell of stale smoke mixed with the itching feeling of fresh smoke in the eyes.

They sat down at the end of the bar, and after the first gulp of an IPA, August poured out his thoughts. "I'm just in the middle of everything and I'm trying to hold everything together. I really am. My wife said she would support me. She just doesn't understand that I'm doing it for her and Jenny. And Dennings doesn't want to understand either. He can't just come and order me to leave my wife simply because she doesn't fit into his master plan. If I have to give them up, what reason do I have to remain in the game?"

Adriana nodded continuously until August had finished. "That's what I told him too, but he was firm with his opinion."

"You knew about this?!" August almost choked.

"The whole inner circle of your campaign does. That's why I wanted to meet with you before..." She bit on the insides of her lips. "I figured at least you deserved a chance to prepare yourself before he told you. You might not believe me, but I care for you."

August didn't reply. He looked at her and ground his teeth until it hurt. Then he exhaled and looked down at the empty beer bottle in front of him. *Why do empty bottles always look sad?* He took a deep breath. *At least she's on my side.*

"I am sorry, August. Jude is not a bad man, he's sorry too, but you have to understand him. You agreed to the plan and there's a lot at stake for the country and The Holding. He's under a lot of pressure too to make this happen."

August looked up again, but his eyes felt empty. "I guess I will lose them anyways, if I haven't already. Things haven't been great lately, you know." He paused to get the words right. "At least this way they wouldn't have to deal with the stress and publicity of being the First Family. They could live a safe and peaceful life without me."

"It sounds as if I you've already decided." Adriana touched his elbow.

August knew she was right, the dice had been thrown. *Funny how fast you can find arguments when you've made up your mind.* "Do you live close by?" August tried to direct the conversation in a different direction.

She smiled. "Do you want to come home with me?"

"That's not what I meant." He was about to take a sip of his beer, but he put the bottle down.

"But that's what *I* meant," she said and set up a smaller version of her smile.

August put on a shy smile. Her offer surprised him, but he wasn't aroused. He was just glad not to be alone. He didn't even care what Olivia might think.

#

August – September 21 – 7 Months to Day 0
(Burlington, VT)

August wished he had taken a coat with him, but then again it would have been difficult to fool the guards when he was being driven around all the time. He was standing under a tree in the old Burlington industrial park, where Niklas lived. All the houses were grey, only here and there weeds grew through the cracks in the cement.

August was shivering; it was freezing for a September evening. *Hope Niklas shows up soon.* He wasn't worried about the guards—who would suspect he was here?—it was just freaking cold, too cold for the usual creepy people in the area to be outside.

A light came on in one of the windows. August looked up, held his breath for a second and then exhaled. *Wrong window.*

August had tried to sneak out of corporate suites before, once in Dallas and once in Chicago; every time he had been caught, but not this time. The roadshow in Vermont had been cancelled and the guards had not yet been informed when he waved at them as the elevator doors closed. He escaped through the hotel kitchen—throwing his watch and Comm-Dongle onto a tray—and once he was out he knew they wouldn't be able to follow him in his own hood. Burlington was his home and he knew all the alleys and back roads.

Light. This time it was the right window.

August peeked left and right. He was still the only soul in the street. He ducked, ran over to the old factory and climbed up the emergency stairs. *The physical training the campaign team set up for me is paying off.* He knocked on the window next to the lit one. *That should be his kitchen—I hope he still lives here.*

"Turn around, slowly," said a voice behind him.

Niklas. August exhaled markedly and turned around.

"Look up."

August looked up. Right beneath the upper level he noticed an old Bluetooth camera. Half a minute later the unlit window opened. August climbed in. The window was closed behind him and the blinds were lowered.

"I'm honored. Why do I deserve a visit from the President of America?"

"I'm not yet elected."

"Come on, you know how the system works." Niklas chuckled.

"Good to see you, man."

They hugged.

"Good to see you. What are you doing here? Need somebody to slap reason into you?"

"I might have needed that a year or two ago." August took a deep breath. His eyes adjusted to the dim light. Niklas' face remained in the dark.

"I might be able to help," said Niklas. "I have cash and a plan to get to South America. And I can make you disappear. You need a new name?"

For the first time in months August chuckled and Niklas joined him. *How I have missed Niklas!*

The chuckling went away and August felt a band tighten around his chest. "Listen, I don't have a lot of time. I need you to look after my family."

"Don't tell me you care now, not after you got rid of them."

"I couldn't stop it. They threatened to arrest them. Jenny is taking part in the Resistance."

"The Resistance?" Niklas seemed to breathe louder. "Did they say which cell?"

"At her college. I need you to get her out of there. Keep her safe. Will you do that for me?"

August could hear Niklas' smile. "That's the least I can do for a friend. You don't want to just run away? The offer for a new name is still there."

"Thank you, but they would punish Olivia and Jenny. Listen, I have to go."

"Take the other stairs. They go into the backyard and from there you can get to the other side of the block."

Niklas led August through the dark loft, opened the window on the other side and peeked out. "All clear. Listen, I never doubted you. I know once they get you they don't let you go. I've got your back."

They hugged and August climbed out of the window. Shortly afterwards he was at the exit of the backyard. He peeked out and turned into the street, smiling peacefully.

CHAPTER TEN

President

August – April 16, 2045 – 5 Days to Day 0 (Washington, CD)

Augugust Remules was elected 49th president of the United States of America with 66% of all votes. He even won five of the deep Democratic states on the East Coast. His rivals had been eliminated during the campaign, one by one, but August had not been surprised by the scandals and uncovered illegal activities. He remembered too well the various candidates they had selected during that week in Fairview and how they had highlighted their weaknesses. One Republican candidate had falsified real-estate contracts, and a candidate of the Democrats had a too-promiscuous life. "Nights were long and cold in Anchorage," August's team had joked. One of August's team had said this was the easiest campaign he had ever participated in; the candidates were falling like turkeys during hunting season.

For only one Democratic candidate had they not been able to prepare anything in their first meetings in Fairview. Even August had been surprised when they had found drugs and child pornography in his apartment. His party dropped him like a hot potato.

Even the fact the August had his own scandals didn't endanger his election. His recent divorce and remarriage would have been unthinkable for a presidential campaign thirty years earlier, but with the right statement and The Holding's media power, the message was hammered in: a president needs a wife who stands behind him, and Adriana Jensen does so without question. August had never commented on the reasons which The Holding blasted out on every occasion. He knew he was only doing it to protect his family, and sometimes that means making the biggest sacrifice yourself.

All these thoughts ran through August's mind while he sat in the eleventh meeting with his cabinet.

A pinching pain went through his heart. He had expected Olivia's tears when he told her about the divorce, but Jenny's anger and hatred killed him every time he thought about it. Her eyes glowed yellow like he had never seen them.

He took a deep breath as if that could blast away the band around his chest.

"Bored, Mr. President?" Vice President McNally's sneering tone brought August back to the cabinet meeting. McNally continued without waiting for August's reaction.

August was used to it. He had had no say in the campaign or the selection of his cabinet, so why should he have any say in here? The business passed him by. The secretaries decided and submitted things for his signature; at the beginning he had tried to read them or insisted on being briefed, but they urged him to sign and said it would be extraneous anyway. One time he had denied his signature, with the result that his Vice President and the Secretary of State had signed in his name, in front of him.

When he had protested, they had cackled, "We can do that now. You signed that law yourself." They walked out waving the e-pad over their heads.

And then there was Adriana, still organizing his meetings and having breakfast and dinner with him, but other than that living a different life. Slowly August realized that she had achieved her goal: she lived in the White House, and as Secretary of National Intelligence she had more power than any First Lady had ever had before.

"You know," he said during one breakfast, "I imagined the office differently: more responsibility, difficult decisions and tough discussions."

Adriana didn't bother to look up.

"Even you are closer to what's going on."

She was still staring into her e-pad.

"You can tell Dennings in your next weekly update that, right now, I sit bored in the Oval Office."

Now she looked up. August wasn't quite able to determine her expression—something between amusement and aggravation.

"Why do you complain?" She squinted harshly. "When was the last time you had enough time to read a book? I would love to have your position and that staff. Your people try to protect you and deal with the adversities of the office. Most of your predecessors would wish they had your life." Adriana rolled her eyes and leaned back. "But if you're really bored, try to use your computer. You have access to everything in there. Order some secret files from the FBI or the NSA."

She stood up and shook her head.

"You're the President, for God's sake," she said with the voice of an angel and the face of a devil before she turned around and walked towards the door. "Enjoy the power a little. You might even be the first president not to look old after the term," she added before she left.

August sat back and grabbed another bagel. *Curious how fast you gain weight when eating remains the only satisfaction in life.* He missed Burlington, Lake Champlain and the trips to the cabin. Roberta flashed through his mind. He wondered what had happened to her.

Later, in the Oval Office, he started his virtual machine and tried to access random information. Adriana was right—it seemed he had access to everything: defense strategies, troop movements, tax information. Everything he tried to access came up. He chuckled and his misery was gone in a moment. He remembered a requirement from the Secret Service he had signed off on Project OneHub: to prevent a coup via IT, the president's access rights were hard-coded.

Roberta was rather easy to find, but the cheer went out of him when he saw the size of the dossier. He flipped through pages and pages of her writing, filled with annotations about her conspiring with anarchists. Somebody had gone to great lengths to frame her as a terrorist. Other parts of the document contained photos of her, in New York, in Europe, in China. August's pulse doubled when he saw a photo of him and Roberta in the Lakeshore coffee shop in Burlington. Seconds later he frowned when he noticed that, instead of the dinner at August's house, they had reported her as having returned to New York. Frantically he scrolled through the rest of the photos and reports, but there was nothing of the dinner in his house or their trip to the cabin. He relaxed a little, but then his eyes opened wide: instead of their trip to the cabin, the report stated that she was travelling abroad during that time. August flipped further through the reports. She had lived under a fake name and they were still investigating how she had got the name into the system. He smirked for a second; she had managed to give them the runaround after all.

August read further and his heart froze when he realized that she was now imprisoned in the high-security prison for terrorists in Palos Verde. The prison was located about thirty miles west of what was left of the nuclear plant of Palos Verde. The area was uninhabitable from the contamination it had suffered after the meltdown of the plant due to the terrorist attack. For most of the prisoners it was like death row, and Roberta had already been there four years, convicted in a summary proceeding.

August leaned back and closed his eyes. He waited a minute until his heartbeat had calmed down before he said, "Call McNally."

"Calling." The AI had a military voice. August had liked Alex's voice much more.

"Office of the Secretary of the Interior, this is Gaby."

"Hi, Gaby, can you put me through to Dave?"

"He's in a meeting. Can I take a message? What is your name, sir?"

"August—"

"I'm so sorry. I didn't recognize you, Mr. President. I'll put you through."

"Mr. President?" McNally's voice sounded annoyed and somehow August liked it.

"I want you to transfer Prisoner ZZ423713Q into a different prison."

August could hear McNally breathing hard.

"I am not sure I understood correctly."

"I want you to transfer a prisoner into a different prison. ZZ423713—"

"That is Secretary Evans' area. I'll have it handed over to him," said McNally swiftly and hung up.

August leaned back and put his feet on the table. *Poor McNally. That must have thrown him off balance.*

In the afternoon, Secretary of the Interior Evans called him.

"Well?" August sneered. *Let's see how they try to get out of this.*

"I was wondering if there is a reason you have taken a specific interest in this prisoner? Usually the president wouldn't handle a single prisoner. It could compromise you if the media noticed it. Did you know her?"

"No, I do not." August felt hot. "Adriana suggested I review some files. The prisoner's sentence doesn't include any charges for terrorism and yet she is being held in a facility dedicated to terrorists. I wonder if there are any other cases like this. However, as a start we should transfer this prisoner to another facility."

"I was indeed wondering that myself, so I checked." Evans made an important pause. "I can confirm we have no other cases like this. Now, regarding the transfer of the prisoner, that won't be possible, I'm afraid. There was a lapse in the process. The record hasn't been updated—staff shortages, you know. The prisoner in question was shot yesterday in a prison revolt..."

August stopped listening. He closed his eyes for a moment and when he opened them again he saw the blue sky above DC. Breathing should be easier with that beautiful weather outside, he thought.

"Sir, are you still there?"

"Yes, thank you for the update, Anthony."

August remained in his chair after he hung up, still looking outside. *Fucking bullshit. They killed her themselves.*

August already had the habit of having a glass of wine in the evening, or sometimes a little more, but this evening he killed two bottles alone.

CHAPTER ELEVEN

Car Keys

Jenny – April 18 – 3 Days to Day 0 (Burlington, VT)

" Nothing's wrong, Eduard. I just had a bad day."

Jenny and Eduard were on their way to Jacob's house for a meeting. They had passed Jacob's house and left Jenny's car further down the road. From there they were walking with their arms linked, but their pace felt out of synch.

"I don't mean today. This has been going on for months now."

"What the heck! I don't know what you're talking about." Jenny unlinked from Eduard.

He stopped and looked at her. "You had two car accidents last year. Whenever we discuss something you're stubborn, unyielding—it doesn't matter if it's about Resistance work or the color of the towels. Your scores have dropped dramatically. Don't get me wrong, it's not the first time you've got a bad grade, but usually you dig yourself into the books to make it up in the next test. I always admired that." He paused for a moment. "And it's been a while since we've been together."

Until that last sentence Jenny had been ready to explode, but that killed her. "I'm just mad. Ever since Dad left us, I'm mad at

179

everything, everybody, all the time." She linked arms with him again and they continued to walk. "Can't we talk tomorrow? I don't want to fight."

"Why do we have to fight at all? Why can't we talk about things like we always did?"

"Tomorrow evening, I promise. Let's go somewhere nice and quiet and we can talk. Not at home—I don't want Mom thinking we have a problem. She has enough sorrows."

Eduard didn't answer for a moment. "Fine, but we must do it."

Jenny was glad they had arrived at Jacob's house and she didn't have to listen further.

The others welcomed them nicely. They had not come to the meetings in Burlington often in the two years since they first met the cell; most of the time Jenny and Eduard participated in the meetings at their colleges. The few times they had met in Burlington, they had made good friends.

Jenny missed Niklas and looked out for him every time they came. Although he had removed himself from the regular meetings, she always hoped he would still show up. But he never did—except for this time.

She could barely stop herself from shouting his name when she spotted Niklas in the room. She ran into his arms. "I was so hoping to see you here! But what are you doing here? Is something wrong? You're making such a serious face."

"I have to talk to you, Jenny. And you, Eduard." Niklas flicked his head to a remote corner of the room. "Let's go over there."

They walked into the corner. It was dark outside the light cone and Niklas' facial expression remained in the twilight.

PEAK DEMOCRACY | 181

"What's the matter?" Eduard shook Niklas' hand and hugged him.

"You have to leave the group and abandon your activities with the Resistance."

Jenny gasped. "But why?" She stepped back from Niklas. *This is a joke. Never!* "No."

"I promised your dad to watch out for you guys."

"You mean the guy who destroyed our family." Jenny clenched her fists and felt the need to punch something.

"He came to me about a year ago. He was devastated. It was the only way he could protect you, but he needed a friend to watch out for you when he couldn't anymore. I'm sorry I didn't tell you earlier, but this is the first meeting we've both participated in since then."

"Oh no." Jenny shook her head violently. "This is just an easy way for him to ease his conscience. That way he can always tell himself he did everything he could."

"He's a good man and he always wanted the best for you and your mother."

"You watch TV, right? You must have missed out on the wedding last year, when he made that bitch the future FLOTUS."

"It's more complicated than that—"

"And a stupid little girl like me would not understand it." Jenny turned around to Eduard, who was standing behind her. "You have nothing to say?" she snapped.

"Of course I'm on your side, but we should hear him out." Eduard's arms dangled.

"What else is there to say?" Jenny turned back to Niklas. "Any message from my *daddy*?"

Niklas dropped his shoulders. "I shouldn't tell you this, but they knew about your engagement with the Resistance at the university and they blackmailed him by threatening to destroy your future. That's why he agreed to run for president in the first place."

"Her dad is the President?" Martin had sneaked up to them in the darkness and overheard the last words. "That's it—we're cooked. If they know about her, they know about us all. There's no way back anymore, only forward. It's time to stand up and fight."

"That's not true." Niklas raised his voice. "They only know about her university activities. The leak must be somewhere there."

Martin sneered. "Ha! There's probably not even a leak. They simply screened her dad's immediate environment, including you as a good friend of the family. I tell you, now is the time because tomorrow we'll be gone."

"At least somebody in here is not as naive as an egg." Jenny's cheeks hurt from chewing on the insides.

"Enough." Jacob stood up. "We shouldn't get ahead of ourselves. We all might want to be more cautious going forward. But I agree with Niklas: Jenny and Eduard should leave the cell. It's too risky now for the rest of us."

"You can't force me to leave." Jenny put her fists on her hips.

Jacob folded his hands as if he wanted to pray. "I understand, but you have to see the greater good we are fighting for. Sometimes some of us have to bear a little more."

"Jenny, we should leave." Eduard touched her elbow.

That took Jenny's breath away. For a moment she wasn't able to talk, but when she started again, she erupted. "I knew you wouldn't stand by me! How could you?" Her fingernails wanted to scratch his face. She turned around and stomped towards the door.

Eduard wanted to follow her but Niklas called him back.

"Wait. There's more I need to tell you."

Jenny turned around, looking at Eduard, who stood in the middle between her and the group.

"Wait one second, Jen. I'll be right with you."

She shook her head and left, more running than walking.

#

Niklas – 3 Days to Day 0

Niklas grabbed Eduard's arm before he could run after Jenny.

"I need to go before she does anything stupid." Eduard tried to shake Niklas off.

"One minute. This is important." Niklas put on his most serious, insistent face.

"Fine." Eduard pulled a face and his gaze went over to the door, which was just closing again. Somebody else must have left.

Niklas came closer. "I've placed an insurance policy in the system in case anything happens to me or Jenny's dad or you guys."

Eduard looked at him with a frown on his face.

"You have to memorize this sequence: 22.65qq.205.ff11.— Eduard, look at me. This can decide life or death."

"I'm listening." Eduard's gaze went up the stairs again. "Can't you write this down?"

"No! You have to remember it. Ff11. and then the word 'scramble'. Can you repeat that?"

"Yeah. 22.65qq.25—"

"No!" Niklas whisper-shouted. "*205*. Again."

"22.65qq.205.ff11.scramble. Niklas, what is that?"

"Shh...!" hissed Niklas and looked around.

The others were staring at them, but they were too far away.

Niklas turned back to Eduard. "Just go with it. I can't tell you any more. If something happens, give it to somebody who understands technology—somebody you trust—and they will know."

Eduard nodded absently, again gazing up the stairs.

"Now, let's get Jenny." Niklas patted Eduard on the back.

They turned around and ran upstairs. When they came out of the house they saw the rear of Jenny's car disappearing around the corner.

"Damn! I shouldn't have listened to you." Eduard poked Niklas in the chest. "If something happens, it's your fault." He pointed at Niklas, turned around and ran in the direction in which the car had disappeared.

#

Jenny – 3 Days to Day 0

Jenny was almost at the garden gate when she heard the door go behind her. She turned around and wanted to say something along the lines of "Don't come with me now, you had your chance," but to her surprise it was Martin who had followed her.

"Listen. I know it sounds crazy, but I have an idea."

She wanted to send him to hell, but her thoughts formed only *To hell.* "And what would that be?"

"If you found your own cell, I'll be your contact person to the net. That way you can still be part of the cause, and the others won't need to know for the moment."

"You would do that?" Jenny pricked up her ears.

He put on a winning smile Jenny didn't know he had. "Absolutely. You are courageous and you have the right spirit. The cause should not lose you."

"I can't do a lot. I'm a one-man show right now."

Martin nodded. "I could use your help, actually."

Jenny raised her eyebrow. "Not sure how I can help you."

"I have to get some stuff for a small task, but it's a little heavy. I'd need your car for the night. You don't have to come with me. I'll just park it in your driveway in an hour or two. Unless you don't want to support me?"

"It's nothing illegal, right?" Jenny frowned.

"You mean outside the fact that it's for the Resistance?" Martin smirked. "No, nothing illegal."

"Okaaay," said Jenny. "But you'll bring it back without a dent."

"Sure," Martin replied as Jenny handed him the car keys.

She turned around without another word and walked home.

CHAPTER TWELVE

The Call

Olivia – April 19 – 2 Days to Day 0 (Burlington, VT)

Olivia woke up late—almost at noon—and immediately wished she hadn't. A horrible headache was throbbing through her temples. She almost knocked the empty wine bottle off the bedside table when she reached for the alarm clock. She sat up. *The kids should not see me like this.* Five throbs later she tried to stand up and managed it on the third attempt. She staggered in slow motion into the bathroom. Why where three of her sleeping pills missing? *I haven't taken three. Jenny must have taken them. Again!*

Olivia felt better after taking a shower, and she was ready to leave her bedroom. The kitchen was empty. Jenny's note from the day before, that they probably would not be home until late at night, was still on the kitchen counter.

Judging from the silence in the house, they're out again.

She wasn't too unhappy about it; that way she didn't have to fake a smile. She switched on the lunchtime news and poured coffee. Somewhere someone had committed an arson attack on an FBI building. They had driven a burning car into the lobby. Oliv-

187

ia threw a glance at the TV—it almost looked like Burlington. Three guards had died. They had also stolen weapons and explosives, but the federal authorities had already picked up four suspects in the night.

The usual suspects. Olivia was fed up of the depressing news and flipped over to some cute puppy videos on a social-media site for pet lovers.

As the drowsiness disappeared, a strange restlessness grabbed her. She got up and started cleaning the fridge, something she had not done since August left. Thinking of August, she realized that she still had a garage full of his stuff. *Away with that crap.* She left the fridge cleaning halfway through, went to the garage and started throwing away his stuff, or rather moving it from left to right so Eduard could throw it out the next day. When she came back into the house she realized that she had left the fridge open. *Damn, now I have to throw away all the food inside.*

Annoyed at herself, she got a glass of wine from the bar and cheese from the fridge. *Hell.* She grabbed the whole bottle and everything that was still tasty out of the fridge, put it on a plate and sat down with a knife on the sofa to watch more puppy videos.

#

The buzz of the communicator woke her up shortly before midnight. At first, she heard only a sobbing at the other end.

"Jenny?" Olivia was wide awake.

"Mom, please come and get me out of here. They took me last night. Eduard too." The last words were eaten by weeping.

"Who? What happened?"

"The FBI. They say we killed people. They're all here; Jacob, Hanna and the others. Only Martin isn't here. Oh my god, it was Martin. He took my car—"

"Jenny? Jenny, are you there?"

The line was dead. Olivia closed her eyes and fell back on the couch. *This can't be.* Her fingers trembled. *Why us? Why always us! Can't we live like any other family?* The throbbing was back and it came with a crystal-clear thought. *It's over. Everything's gone.* She opened her eyes again and looked at the ceiling. It was moving away and Olivia expected any second to hit the ground, but she didn't. At some point—she wasn't able to say if it was after seconds, minutes or hours—she was back. She blinked twice, clenched her fists and grabbed the home communicator to call the local police.

Chief Matthews picked up.

"Ken, this is Olivia. My daughter just called to tell me that she's been arrested. There must be a mistake."

"Unfortunately this is correct, Olivia. I'm sorry." The chief had put on an unusually formal voice.

"Under what charges?" She clamped her hand around the armrest of the sofa.

"I am not permitted to tell you, but you can call the FBI hotline tomorrow morning. They might be able to tell you more."

"I'm coming down to the station." Olivia sat up and was about to get up.

Chief Matthews took a breath. "You can certainly do so, but they are being transferred as we speak."

"Transferred? Where?" Her heart froze.

"I don't know. But even if I knew, I could not tell you."

"How can that be? She has the right to a lawyer." Olivia's voice was close to shrieking.

He paused. "Not for what she did."

"What does that mean? What did she do?"

"I really can't tell you, Olivia. You have to call the FBI hotline."

"Tell me!" Olivia's voice got shrill.

Chief Matthews swallowed. "Don't blame me. I let her call you because we're friends. That alone could get me in trouble."

Olivia let the home communicator slide out of her hand. She looked into the mirror. She looked pale, almost ashen. After a second she looked around frantically. *There must be something, anything I can do*. She picked up the communicator and threw it against the wall. The thud didn't help. She grabbed a heavy book and threw it against the mirror. The shattering sound helped a little.

Her eyes fell on the knife on the coffee table. She took it and a hot, sharp pain flooded through her as she cut herself on the outside of her arm. *Finally feeling something*. It was only a small cut and she couldn't resist cutting a second time and then once more. After the seventh cut she realized what she was doing and rushed into the bathroom to clean the wounds. When she came out of the bathroom she had a sloppy bandage around her arm and she stood still for a moment. She rushed into Jenny's bedroom and looked around as if the solution would be hidden somewhere there. Several times she turned around. All the good memories from Jenny's childhood passed in front of her eyes and she threw up in the middle of the room. As if she had needed that to come to her senses, she knew what to do. *I'll sit in front of their offices until they answer me.* She took an ice-cold shower, attended to her wounds more diligently, got dressed and left.

#

August – 2 Days to Day 0 (Washington DC)

Since hearing about Roberta, August had decided it was time to take action. Finally he felt taken seriously, something he had not felt since the first time he had been to Fairview. He called a staff meeting and everybody came. Maybe it had something to do with his threat that everybody who did not appear could hand in their resignation. The arson attack on the FBI building in Burlington had put the whole country in shock. The *New York Times* called for hard and fast measures from the President. Every news station was asking for answers and action, and August was ready to give it to them. His staff tried to convince him that it was better not to overreact and simply to put the terrorists away; the terror laws would allow that without a court ruling if the President had enough evidence. But August wanted more. He had found an angle and now he ordered a complete investigation into the attack, the background and how the Resistance could be defeated. He didn't really care how to defeat the Resistance, but it would keep his staff them on the back foot for months. With a certain satisfaction he observed that the Secretary of Defense was looking twitchily at the Vice President, but McNally remained calm—at least he appeared that way on the outside.

"We will get right on it, Mr. President."

August squinted at McNally. "I can assume you already have some intel? I'll expect your first reports tomorrow morning."

After everybody had left the Oval Office, August looked out of the window and clapped his hands. Finally he was there. As he

192 | G.D. LEON

left the Oval Office he noticed that McNally, Evans and Adriana were debating at the end of the hallway. It almost seemed like they were fighting, August thought with a smirk. He didn't have to go that way, but he wanted to see if they would stop and leave if he came closer. They did and August had to suppress a laugh.

#

Olivia – April 20 – 1 Day to Day 0

Olivia reached DC at sunrise and got into rush hour; more than once she had to slam on the brakes to avoid a crash. "Freaking snails!" she shouted at the other cars, ignoring the constant blaring of her own collision system.

Throughout the whole trip she had tried to reach people on her Comm-Dongle—August, Jenny and August again—but nobody had picked up. In her desperation, Olivia had grabbed at every straw she could think of. She even tried to reach Amnesty International in Canada, but the number was blocked in the USA. She wished she had paid more attention when the NGOs were bullied out of country a decade ago. *I never thought I would miss them.*

The lines were moving slower than walking pace. She gasped for air and her hands clamped around the steering wheel.

Finally Niklas picked up. "Yes?"

"Niklas?! Oh my god, Niklas, I'm so happy to reach you." She almost cried.

"What's wrong? You sound awful."

"I'm sorry to call you and I know I should have called you back last week, but I'm desperate."

"What happened?" Niklas' voice turned worried.

"They've arrested Jenny. They wouldn't tell me why. I'm on my way to the FBI in DC."

Niklas didn't reply.

"Are you still there?" Olivia felt her breath stumble.

"Yes."

"I need your help." Olivia had a difficult time stopping the car moving with her trembling.

"What can I do? I'm not a lawyer."

"I don't know. Something. Call August."

"I don't think August will be reachable. I'm sorry, I really don't see how I can help you."

This time Olivia was speechless.

"I hope everything clears up. Bye, Olivia."

Olivia closed her eyes and almost bumped into the car ahead of her. *No car crash now*. Moving far too slowly, she continued to call numbers, hoping that one of them would help her—at least more than Niklas. She honked at the car in front that wouldn't move despite almost a yard of space.

Nobody picked up on August's personal number. *Hell, this is part of the divorce agreement. You have to be reachable for family matters. Anytime*. She could buy a gun and press them out. *No, the FBI would never agree to that. They would smile at me before a sniper's bullet hit me*. She had seen that on the news.

The FBI hotline still had the automatic voice telling her that they were facing a lot of calls and suggesting she go to the nearest FBI service desk. *Cheap bastards—they don't even let the AI run 24/7. Give them bread and circuses and they're too lazy to move their asses*. She dialed a different number.

"The White House, this is Lindsey, how can I help you?"

"Good lord, you're finally there! I already tried multiple times."

"I'm sorry, ma'am, our business hours are 7AM to 7PM. How can I help you?"

"I need to talk to August Remules. It's urgent. It's about his daughter."

"I'm sorry, ma'am, I can't connect you to the President. But I can give you somebody from his staff."

"You don't get it, it's an emergency. I'm his ex-wife and his daughter has... Just tell his staff or whoever that it's urgent."

"I understand, Ms. Remules. Please hold for a moment."

Remules—pronounced in French? That was a freaking AI.

The car in front of her changed lanes. *I'm glad I don't have a gun.*

"Hello."

"This is Olivia Remules, August Remules' ex-wife. You need to put me through to him. It's about his daughter and it's really urgent."

"Hi, Olivia, this is Adriana. Good to hear from you again."

Olivia had a taste of blood and bile in her mouth. "His daughter got arrested for the terror attack this morning. She had nothing to do with it."

"I know. August was devastated." Adriana had an overly sweet tone in her voice that made Olivia want to kill her.

"He has to get her out." Olivia's hands clamped around the steering wheel.

"How should he do that? You have to understand, Olivia."

The sweetness in Adriana's voice just got too much for Olivia and she closed her eyes. She opened them again when the alert system in her car beeped to tell her that the lines were moving, just before the car behind her honked.

"Honey, he can't just get somebody out. But I am sure everything will clear up as she's innocent."

"Why can't you let her out if you know she's innocent?"

Adriana was quick with an answer, as if she had prepared for it. "We are still investigating. I'm sorry, but listen: call me next week and we might be able to tell you more. Just call the main line and ask for Adriana."

"But—"

Adriana was quick again. "I have to run. It was nice talking to you. Bye."

The line went dead.

Bitch! If I had a gun now, I would kill her.

Olivia sheared off to cut off a car that wanted to pass on the shoulder. An extended honking was the result.

"Bitch," Olivia said out loud, looking in the rearview mirror. *No, they won't get my daughter. I will not let that happen.*

She reached the parking downtown.

I should still be early enough, she thought. *Probably I'm the first, or among the first.*

She rushed straight to the FBI Museum and Information building, through the building entrance and towards the information desk, but she didn't get far. Turning around the last corner, she froze. She found herself at the end of the line. The service and information desk was about 500 feet away, at the end of a broad hallway full of waiting people. She could hear the loud voices of people arguing with FBI employees behind bulletproof glass. She didn't understand what they were saying, but from their gestures she guessed they had moved over into insults. A guy fainted and heavily armed security guards dragged him through a side door. He was covered in blood.

After a few seconds Olivia was able to move again and she stood in line. At first she didn't look at the others. She didn't want to have any contact and, even more, she didn't want to talk about why she was here. But as minutes passed without movement she looked at the people around her. It was quiet and only further down could she see people talking to each other. Even further down the talking seemed to merge into one large discussion, just to become quiet again shortly before the bulletproof glass. She realized that she'd be here for the rest of the day, but the unbearable consequences gave her a stoic calmness. She would endure everything to save her child.

#

Niklas – 1 Day to Day 0 (Burlington, VT)

Enough... is... enough!

Olivia's call had left Niklas with a strange feeling of detachment. He felt bad for cutting her off, but he could not talk on that phone line. For the first three minutes his thoughts dripped. Sluggishly the idea ripened of how he could save them. *The only two truly innocent people.* He had the power to undo things, but that wouldn't help here; the whole world would know them, so maybe the world should forget everything else.

Tonight, tonight, but I need prep time. Niklas walked over to his supervisor's desk. "John, I don't feel that well. Can we switch shifts? I could take over your night shift. I know you have your monster day today with afternoon and night shift together."

Niklas' manager grunted without looking up. "So, what's her name?"

"Olivia," Niklas lied.

Now he looked up. "*That* Olivia? No way! What would you be then? Almost-FLOTUS cuckold?"

"Not that Olivia."

"Ok, well, I don't care. I'm actually not too unhappy with that, but be here on time."

Niklas was sweating when he got into his car, and he stopped for a moment. In his thoughts he went through the list he had prepared uncountable times. *First, get my escape ready—they will hunt me the moment I start this.*

The routines were in place and just needed to be kicked off. He already had John's password for the second approval: 'Jessica'. In his mind he went through his vault: $50,000 in cash, twenty tiny gold bars, three watches and other small valuables to trade in later. *I still need outdoor gear. Guess I can buy that on card. It won't matter anymore.* He chuckled. *And then I need more cash to get the illegal stuff.*

Three hours later he had $4,000 in cash from five banks; he could not get more without raising flags. He also had the outdoor stuff and durable food and was ready to get the *delicate* supplies next.

He went to the deli around the corner from where he had lived years ago. It was deserted that early in the afternoon. There was only the owner, lounging in his chair and watching TV.

"What's up, Dan?" Niklas said.

"Well, well, look who's here. The lost son." The storeowner got up and his hand went underneath the counter, reaching for the gun. "Are you alone?"

Niklas saw the movement and remained in the door with his hands raised a little to show that they were empty. "I thought I'd visit my old friend."

"Right." He got up and peeked at the door. His hand went back to the counter when he saw nobody else was coming in.

"I'm glad your deli is still running well."

Dan looked around the empty store. "Right."

"Listen, do you still have your... specialties?" Niklas looked around as well, as if the specialties were something Dan would place in plain sight.

"Sure, here is the light beer, over there is the milk, and the pizza is in the freezer." Dan chuckled.

Niklas lowered his head and looked up at Dan. "I'm serious."

Dan nodded slowly. "Right."

"Listen, I have cash." Niklas grabbed a roll of banknotes out of his pocket and waved it in front of Dan's face. Dan raised an eyebrow and went to the door. He glanced out of the small window in the door and then put up a sign that read, 'Be right back'.

"So, you got cash." He dawdled back towards Niklas.

"I need gear. Body-heat repellent, water sanitizer, night goggles, a non-traceable GPS and a non-standard stun gun that works against the bulletproof vests of the police." Niklas withstood Dan's stare.

After a second, Dan blew out air, looked down and back up. "Wow, wow, wow. That's it? Nothing more? I'm sure you know of my obligation to report you. Just the mere fact that you asked for these things raises the obligation."

Niklas knew Dan was teasing him. Years ago, when Niklas had lived around here, Dan had bragged that he could get anything. "I need you not to report me. I can trust you on this, right? You owe me, or shall I call you by your real name, Henry?"

"Maybe—"

"If not for me and Jacob, you would be in Palos Verde right now. Unjustified, but still." Niklas opened his arms.

"—maybe not, but I think the money in your hand is not enough to get all this stuff."

"I have more."

"How much?"

"Two grand," said Niklas.

"That could be enough for most of it, but not for the stun gun. They're expensive."

"What's expensive?"

"1,000 more."

"Ok, here you go." Niklas put $3,000 on the table.

Dan grunted. "You didn't kill somebody, did you?" He eyed Niklas. "Never mind. Come with me."

They went into the freezer room, where Dan opened a hatch between two boxes. Behind the door, smaller boxes were piled up. He grabbed two of the smaller boxes and gave them to Niklas. Niklas glanced at the contents and handed him the cash.

"Always nice to do business with you." Dan grinned when they came back to the front of the store. Niklas didn't reply and walked towards the door.

"Tell me, Niklas, why do you need all this stuff?" He paused. "Actually, I don't want to know, but I'd suggest you grab one of those empty wine boxes over there."

Niklas nodded and left the deli with a box of cheap wine from Patagonia.

CHAPTER THIRTEEN

Death Sentence

August – 1 Day to Day 0 (Washington DC)

August would not have signed the death sentence if he had known. But he did and he did it in a statesmanlike manner. Adriana brought him the papers that needed the presidential signature: two new bills to sign, a small reorganization in the Ministry of Defense, a birthday card for the Prime Minister of Japan and the death sentence for the terrorists responsible for the Burlington multiplex arson attack.

"The reports this morning were promising. I didn't expect you to get them that quickly. But I didn't see their names." August handed back the paper he had just signed.

Adriana's face showed no reaction. "They're in the death sentence order you just signed."

August took the papers back and looked through them.

"There are only prisoner numbers. I don't want to read their names in the newspaper tomorrow, like last time I signed a death sentence and it turned out to be a famous artist."

"The translation is in my office. I'll get it for you."

Adriana wanted to take the papers, but August didn't let go.

"We need to get it executed. It's lined up for communication for tomorrow's news," she insisted.

"You will execute them today?"

"No, but within forty-eight hours. They will be transferred to Palos Verde today. That way we can issue several bulletins over the next two days to feed the news with details. It's good for your reputation. I will send you the names, I promise."

August squinted and grunted after a moment. *I really got them.* He chuckled.

"I am also still waiting for the second part of the report: how to defeat the Resistance."

"We are working on it," said Adriana. She grabbed the papers and left.

#

Niklas – 1 Day to Day 0 (Burlington, VT)

After Niklas reached home that afternoon he checked everything and packed it into his old kit bag. *Now the only thing left is to deceive them,* he thought. He started his e-pad and booked a flight to the Bahamas with one of the low-cost airlines for the next morning. Niklas looked at his watch: only one hour until his shift started. He looked around his apartment. No, there was nothing he would miss. He grabbed his kit bag and left for the office. Better to be early, especially as he wanted to get gas.

He arrived right on time at the multiplex building. On the other side of the Shelburne Bay he could see the damaged FBI building. *The security guards will know—they're trained to notice abnormal behaviour.* His hands trembled when he passed the security gate. *Any second they'll storm out and catch me.*

Nothing happened.

"Good evening, Mr. Soderstrom," said a friendly voice and the gates opened.

The operations control room was empty when the elevator doors opened ten levels below ground. John had already left. Leaving early wasn't allowed, but it wasn't the first time his manager had taken a French leave.

Niklas checked his watch: 6PM. He would be alone until 8PM when the building security would start their hourly checks. They were not allowed to enter the room, but they would glance out of the elevator into the room. Two hours—that was plenty of time to start the scrambling routine and let it develop before anybody would notice it. Niklas had classified the routine as an anti-malware patch; that way it would be distributed to all data centers with highest priority. The routine would use the first back-door entry as well as Niklas' second back-door entry to randomly scramble data on three data centers simultaneously, changing it forever. Niklas only needed the access credentials of three people for that.

It's always astonishing how stupid people are, he thought with a smirk. John had found a way to bypass the biometric login and replace it with a simple password, and for days after he had bragged about it and the rest of the team had adopted it. Niklas grinned. *Lazy bastard—one login step vs two login steps with the biometrics login.* All Niklas needed to do was open his coworkers' top drawers and he had his access codes. Who would expect a password in plain sight when everything was supposedly secured with an iris scan?

Before he got into the routine, he logged in as John and booked three tickets to China for the coworkers whose logins he would use. Then the moment came. Niklas took a deep breath, glanced around and started the scramble routine. He got up and confirmed the command at the two coworkers' stations. A simple 'Routine started' message appeared on the screen, and a feeling of both relief and anxiety grabbed Niklas.

#

Olivia – April 21, 2045 – Day 0 (Washington DC)

Olivia saw it on the news. The day before, she had reached the middle of the line when the desk closed and everybody had to leave. After a short night, Olivia got up at 3AM just to be in line in front of the FBI Museum and Information building at 4AM. There were already about thirty people ahead of her. After a while the woman next to her offered her some coffee. She declined at first, but then she changed her mind and was glad afterwards to have something warm in her hands.

"Why are you in line, if I may ask?" said the woman.

"Looking for my daughter. She was arrested yesterday even though she's innocent."

"It's a shame," said a man next to the woman.

"And you? It seems you're better prepared than me." Olivia pointed to the coffee and the sandwiches they had with them.

"Our son went missing a month ago and so far we've found out that the FBI has taken him into custody. They accused him of being here illegally, but he was born in the US. Since then we've been coming every day. It doesn't help, but what else can we do?" The man shrugged his shoulders, but Olivia could hear the scratching in his voice.

During the next hours she learned a lot of different voices. The stories followed a similar pattern. Innocent people, mainly kids in their early twenties, were arrested for nothing and held without information, much less a fair trial—and all under the anti-terror laws of 2030. It seems this had been going on for years; under the radar of public knowledge.

When the doors opened at 8AM the line behind Olivia had grown to over 200 people. By then security guards had already checked her three times and they had removed six people ahead of her. It was almost her turn when she saw the news on the screens along the walls.

She fell.

#

August – Day 0 (Washington DC)

August had woken up at 7AM—earlier than usual. He knew they called him the 'late-riser president', but he didn't care. After a nice shower he sat down in his bathrobe for breakfast. The news was already pre-loaded on his e-pad and as he read he reached out for the coffee mug.

The mug fell.

CHAPTER FOURTEEN

Chaos

Niklas – Day 0 (Burlington VT)

It had been Niklas' longest night and it felt like the coldest down here yet. Relief had given way to anxiety to the point that he had jumped up and walked around the room. His steps on the tiled floor echoed from the naked walls of the empty room.

What have I done? Niklas walked two steps, walked to his desk again and sat down. *How can I reverse it?* The more he realized that it could not be reversed, the more he calmed down. *It's done. There's no way back.* The scrambling had started. It would switch data within the datasets: e-mail addresses, social security numbers, GPS locations, words in texts, contract IDs, biometric data. Niklas had also planted few Easter eggs; a sub-routine of his program would spread the money in a bank equally among all accounts, while another part would change the sequence of presidents, and the most important part would scramble the list of prison inmates—as if he had envisioned Jenny's capture.

Niklas had always been well aware that scrambling the data would not be enough. The protocols and logs would have made it easy to reconstruct everything, but his log adjustment and scrambling routine would make the logs useless.

His last step was to alter his own data. Then everything would be accomplished.

Niklas took a deep breath and jumped to his feet. *Have I forgotten something? No, I haven't. Sure?*

"Ok," he said out loud. *They will be able to narrow down the suspects pretty quickly. I will be the only one gone, so they will look for me. I give them twenty hours, thirty hours max. They will find my car on the bottom of Lake Champlain, but they will neither know my car nor will they have a photo of me.*

"Everything all right, sir?" asked the security guard from the elevator.

"Um, yeah, thank you."

"Ok. Goodnight, sir."

"Goodnight." Niklas sat down again. *Ok, where was I? Any biometric grid search will be useless. I'll have arrived at my refuge before they can dig out any reasonable old-school method.* He smirked again. A message on his screen showed him that phase two of the scrambling routine had started: mixing up the access rights. He typed in the sequence he had given to Eduard—22.65qq.205.ff11.scramble—and a screen with a log appeared. Line after line was added. *Perfect, the scrambling log in the moon data center works smoothly.*

Now he had to act fast before it hit him. He deactivated the government emergency plan, sealed off his virtual machine on the server and bypassed the screen to a simulation.

It will take years to reconstruct the data. Meanwhile, normal life will start again with an equality of opportunity that has never existed before. He would have loved to see the US become the land of unlimited possibility again, but some people have to sacrifice themselves for the greater good.

The employee on the day shift was late. Niklas almost died waiting.

"Sorry for being late, my alarm didn't work."

"No worries, all calm here."

"Out there it's not calm at all. Everybody is crazy today. Is it a full moon?"

"No clue. Listen, I've got to go. See you tonight."

"Bye."

#

Olivia – Day 0 (Washington DC)

Olivia woke up hours after her collapse in a hospital. She didn't say a word, not to the nurses, not to the doctors, not to the psychologist, not to the priest. She sat there, looking out the window without seeing, through the whole day and the entire night. She didn't even notice when the noise in the hospital got louder and louder and a strange atmosphere spread among the staff.

Olivia stood up without looking around her, put on her clothes on and left the hospital. Nobody noticed her in the disorder. On her side, she did not notice that the chaos did not stop at the hospital doors. Traffic lights and traffic were going crazy, the subway was not running and the big advertisement screens were black. Olivia walked to her car and drove off. *West, whatever.*

#

August – Day 0 (Washington DC)

August recovered faster than Olivia. After two bourbons he grabbed his communicator and called the operator with trembling hands.

"Yes, sir, how c—"

"Give me McNally or Evans!"

"One second, please. Their assistants let me know that both are travelling and can't be reached."

"Can't be reached? This is a conspiracy!" August breathed hard. "Treason!" He swallowed. "Tell their assistants I want them to call me within twenty-five minutes or I will dissolve the whole cabinet."

August rushed for the door without caring about his unshaved appearance. *Adriana is in on this.*

Adriana's office was one level down in a quiet corner of the White House. August almost suspected she would be away too; he was surprised when she was there. The door was ajar and he heard her saying she needed her car, immediately. When he rushed into the room, he almost fell over her suitcase. Adriana was sitting behind her large mahogany desk; even the massive golden paperweight looked tiny on that desk. Her eyes opened wide when August stormed into the room.

"How could you? How? You knew it!"

"Knew what?" she evaded.

"You gave me the papers to sign yourself. You knew it! You have to fix it."

"I don't understand." Adriana tried to smile.

"Don't play innocent here." August pounded his fist on the wall. "I know what kind of sneaky bitch you are. You had me send my own daughter to the electric chair!" he yelled.

"It was not my idea. McNally only informed me after the fact. What should I have done?" She blinked as rapidly as she spoke.

"How about letting me know! How about fixing it!" August took a step towards Adriana.

She went pale and tapped on her Comm-Dongle. "Security, please come to my office. I am being threatened."

No answer.

"It seems there's nobody there to help you. No way out this time." August sneered.

Adriana tried to calm her heavy breathing. She moved one hand beneath the desk.

"That was so stupid of you. Now you've lost all leverage over me. You've set me free. I can do what I want." His sneer broadened to a grin. A rare ease came over him.

Adriana narrowed her eyebrows briefly and said with a smug smile, "They will be executed within the usual forty-eight hours. We're not that stupid, you know."

August clenched his teeth, but he didn't feel the pain. "I don't care. I want you to undo it. Go to McNally or whoever and issue a statement that it was an error and they will be released."

"Not going to happen. You know that. Especially as we have proof she did it."

"That's a lie. Like everything you say. Fake." August looked around him. "All this is fake."

"Did you actually read the report? Or did you just sign it in your childish rush to feel important?"

"How stupid of me to believe you got all this information within 24 hours. You must have known it and let it happen on purpose."

Now Adriana smirked. "You have no clue. That's so pathetic." She leaned back, still keeping one hand beneath her desk. "We had a mole in the Burlington cell. They had this IT guy bragging that he could alter data. We only had to take the cell out."

"As I said, you let it happen on purpose. And now you're letting my daughter bleed for it. I hate you for that and I can tell you one thing: watch your back from now on."

"From who? You? Now you've turned from pathetic to embarrassing. You're so stupid it's not even funny anymore."

August took another step towards Adriana. She jumped up and pointed a gun at him that she had been holding beneath her desk. He stopped at the corner of the desk.

"Not one more step. You know what? I'll tell you the truth, just to amuse myself."

August's teeth were grinding and his eyes were fixated on the gun. His brain was calculating the different ways to get around the massive desk.

"We didn't know your brat of a daughter would be involved, but when an opportunity came up, our mole jumped at it. Yes, you heard right, it was our mole that placed the bomb and your little girl was stupid enough to lend him her car."

August's muscles tensed up.

"Don't. I will shoot you," Adriana said with a cold voice.

"You wanted us to defeat the Resistance? Hilarious." She threw her head back. "The government founded the Resistance and McNally is its famous Leader. When the economy didn't get back on track after the financial crisis thirty years ago, the general mood began to boil. The old tactics of using wars abroad to control the people did not work anymore. They became too expensive and the enemies too blurry. That's when McNally and Evans came up with the best vision they could ever have. They let me in on it yesterday. Ingenious: the Resistance channels the emotions and at the same time we gather information about its members to single out the bad apples. McNally... *we* have a mole in every damn cell from here to Corpus Christi. And you know what they told me too? If you ever found out, they would deal with you. I just have to tell them you know and they'll cover for me." She threw her head back, laughing.

August took a stride forward. Adriana targeted August's chest with the gun and her eyebrows narrowed again, but before she pulled the trigger August jumped aside. She shot and missed. He grabbed the heavy nameplate from her desk and threw it at her. Adriana ducked, but by the time she came up again August was already next to her, and he hit her with the golden paperweight from the desk. Then he took the gun and aimed at her.

Adriana was lying groggily on the floor, holding her head with bloody hands. August pressed his lips together, his finger on the trigger and pictures of Jenny in his head, when the scene gained a strange taste.

They set this up. McNally, Evans... Dennings. They want me to kill her. It flashed through August's mind. *No, that makes no sense. They're aiming at Dennings and the power of The Holding. He introduced me. This way they can get rid of me, Adriana and Dennings at the same time.* He took a step towards Adriana, hit her again with the handle of the gun and left the office.

#

As soon as August was back in his room, he got dressed; he wouldn't make a good runaway in a bathrobe. While putting his pants on he dialed with his Comm-Dongle.

"A helicopter, ready to take off as soon as possible."

"I'm sorry, sir, but helicopter rides need to be approved by Homeland Security," said a military voice on the other end of the line.

"Let me guess, McNally has not yet called." August sneered.

"No, sir, he is still travelling."

August's sneer disappeared. "As I thought. Nevertheless, have a helicopter ready asap." August grabbed a used shirt, not letting go of the Comm-Dongle.

"I'm sorry, sir, but it needs authorization by Homeland Security. Even if you were the President, I could not order one."

August paused for a second and replied in his most authoritarian voice, "I am the President."

"Please... I apologize," stammered the man on the other side of the line. "I didn't recognize you. Let me check."

August looked into his wallet. Fifty dollars in cash, his driver's license and tons of cards. *That's not a lot.* He would probably have to go to an ATM.

"Mr. President?" said the male voice through the speaker of the Comm-Dongle.

"Is my helicopter ready?"

"Unfortunately not. The Secret Service needs more time to prepare for a ride. Due to the absence of several cabinet members, we do not have enough agents on call for an additional leave. However, we could arrange for it tomorrow."

August yelled. "Not acceptable. What would you do if I needed to go to the hospital? I need that ride now."

"I understand, Mr. President, but we also need the authorization from Homeland Security. We are still on Threat Level Orange. I hope you understand, sir."

"No, I don't. I'm the President for heaven's sake." August was having problems breathing.

"Yes you are, sir. But you could be being blackmailed or hijacked. These rules are here to protect you."

August hung up without answering. In the meantime he got a small sports bag packed. *I need to get out before Adriana comes round,* he thought feverishly. *Adriana's car! That's it!*

He rushed back to Adriana's office and was glad she was still knocked out. He grabbed the car keys and her badge from her bag. Then he looked around, crushed her Comm-Dongle on the desk and dragged her into the bathroom they had built in for her. Before he left the office, he switched on the 'Do not disturb' sign and locked the office from the outside. *I should have done this before. I got lucky nobody saw her.*

The car was still standing in the driveway. It was her Mustang, the one with the tinted glass, the special rims—and untraceable. Adriana had even passed up on the usual digital comforts, including the GPS locator that all presidential cars were required to have. *She really gets away with everything, that bitch. I bet McNally doesn't even know about this.*

Nobody held him back, neither when he got into the car nor at the gate. Adriana had given an order that nobody was to stop or even check her when she came or went in that car. The car had one of those vintage navigation systems and August made sure not to use the interstates. He ran into two dead ends, but shortly before 11AM he was outside DC.

#

August – April 22 – Day 1 (Palos Verde, AZ)

August drove the whole afternoon and through the night, except for two stops to get gas. At first he had planned to go to an ATM to get cash, but then he found $120,000 in small bills in a sack behind the driver's seat. Clearly Adriana had planned to escape.

At 8AM the next morning, August passed the border between Arkansas and Oklahoma at Fort Smith. Not that this would have been spectacular, but the navigation system beeped and announced that he had arrived at Feldkirch, Austria. August didn't even know where that was, but the arrival beep brought him out of the overtired driving trance he had fallen into. At Roland, Oklahoma he got off the highway to get coffee, but to his surprise only a Coffee&Beans was open, with a quite a crowd inside. August put on his baseball cap and entered the shop.

"...incredible. Nothing works. I'm glad these guys are open," he overheard one man say.

"I even heard they had to break in," replied another. "I tell you, it's this electronics stuff."

After a moment, August relaxed. Nobody would recognize him in here. Thirty minutes later he was back on the road again with a coffee and a bagel. He was glad to be moving, but the incident in the coffee shop had sharpened his senses again and he noticed an increasing number of unusual situations. The traffic lights were switched off, he noticed people on the sides of the roads with open maps on their hoods, and there was only white noise on the radio. The traffic lights and the people puzzled him and the missing music started to worry him. He was certain something was wrong when he passed the border of the 100-mile quarantine zone around Palos Verde, south of Flagstaff. There were no guards, the gates were open and nobody was there to hold him up. He had seen numerous TV documentaries about the aftermath of the terrorist attack and how the government had secured the area after the nuclear meltdown. The only security measures necessary were guards and a complete lockdown on human entry, except for the inmates of the underground prison. It was a strange feeling, driving on that beautiful day through the deserted suburbs and downtown of what had been Phoenix.

He was only stopped when he was almost at the tunnel entrance that led to the gates deep inside the mountain. A vehicle that looked like a mix between a lunar truck and a tank intercepted him, and two heavily armed men in exoskeletons and hazmat suits exited. They had no other choice but to take him in. Instead of letting him through the main gate, he was guided into the area for new inmates.

He had to take a shower and he got new clothes, because of the contamination, they explained. The word 'contamination' made August nauseous. He was allowed to go the bathroom, but he barely made it to the stall before he had to throw up. When he woke up again he was lying on the floor with a horrible headache. He couldn't have been passed out for long as the guards hadn't come for him yet. August got up and washed his face, but the dizziness didn't go away. When he left the bathroom he tried not to stumble too much, but the guards threw looks at each other. They brought him to an interrogation room, where a low-ranking officer was already waiting on him. It cost August some time to talk to the low-ranking officers and go through several identification procedures, most of which did not work, until they believed him to be the President. Finally, the Warden showed up.

"I am devastated, Mr. President," he said. "We have heavy system problems which have caused a prison revolt, the first one in years, but we have been able to bring the old systems back up again. Soon we will have control back. But let's go to my office."

The Warden led him out of the interrogation room and down some emergency stairs, followed by a platoon of prison guards. Walking was easier now and August noticed that he didn't feel that dizzy anymore.

"I wish your visit had been announced. We would have advised you to visit at a later time."

"This is an unplanned visit. I was at an important convention in Las Vegas when my security detail faced technical issues. I decided to travel incognito. The blocked security detail was a perfect target."

"A brave decision, sir."

"It was pure math."

Six floors further down, after they had reached the bottom of the stairs, they walked through a maze of supporting corridors.

"As soon as we have the communication server up again we must call for medical support. The contamination outside can be lethal and our capabilities for the necessary decontamination have been compromised."

August nodded. It seemed as if the Warden had something else on this mind. At a crossing of two corridors, the Warden stopped and turned towards August. He looked at August as if he was in pain.

"It's lucky we have you here with us."

"Why so?"

The Warden walked on again. "We received orders last night to immediately execute the death sentences of the terrorists responsible for the Burlington arson attack. I have to admit that I applaud you. It was a courageous decision to convict your own daughter. You are a true patriot, sir."

"And how can I be of help with this?" asked August, feeling the sweat running down his back.

"Due to the system breakdown, we've lost communication with the mainframe. We will get the revolt under control; we switched off the cooling and the ventilation in the cell area. In twenty-four hours they will fall like ripe apples into our hands. However, without the mainframe we are not able to identify the terrorists, but it is crucial for our track record here that we execute on time and we are already delayed. The people of America rely on us."

"So you will string them along the wall and I'll identify my daughter," asked August with his eyebrows lifted. *How can I sentence my own daughter, moron?* They were now climbing another staircase.

"Not at all, I would not dare ask you to face them. We take photos of all inmates on arrival. However, before the communication broke down, everything got mixed up. We still have the data, but the pictures are wrong."

They arrived at the top of the stairs and entered a room which seemed to be a gear room for the guards. The air was much better here and the damp heat was being blown away by the air conditioning.

"Would you help us?"

"Sure. It's a pleasure for me." August smiled. Idiot.

"Thank you so much, sir."

A security guard opened the door on the other side of the room as if August's answer was a password he had needed to get in.

"Welcome," the Warden said with a hint of pride. "We had to install some conveniences as we get only little free time outside the zone."

They passed a lounge area with a bar, a pool table and an air hockey table. Behind a screen August could see a basketball court and a bowling alley. Even the cafeteria was more like a five-star hotel than a prison.

"We also have a movie theater and a workout room. These men are risking their lives and we owe them the amenities. That way, please."

After they passed a hallway of offices, the Warden and August entered the control center. People were running around and August could smell the sweat and adrenaline in the room. Eight stations were manned. On the large screen, August noticed gunfire and a small explosion, but it was hard to make out anything in the smoke. The Warden made a sign and the picture changed.

One of the stations was cleared for August and he started flipping through the pictures.

"Please let me know when you need a break," said the Warden.

"How many are there?" August asked.

"Well, we have about 3,000 inmates here from the age of fourteen to eighty-five. Unfortunately we can't narrow down the sample due to the mix-up of the data."

After an hour August had looked through 600 pictures and was tired. A picture every six seconds was a good average, but for the others it seemed to be far too slow. The Warden became more and more nervous with every hour that passed, until August shouted after three and a half hours, "There she is."

August was looking at a picture of a young woman with a shaved head and a pitiful look in her eyes. He had never seen her before and for a second he felt guilty. Jenny's picture had passed two hours ago and Eduard's about half an hour ago. Both times August had flipped to the next photo and kept a straight face.

"Now we only have to find the lover," said the Warden with a sweaty smirk.

About half an hour later August found a pretty good match. The Warden was delighted. August was exhausted and happy when he was assigned a sleeping quarters.

The moment he closed the door behind him the nausea came back. He puked a mix of green bile and red blood. It scared him a little—he had never puked blood—but he felt a little better afterwards. He washed his mouth and went to sleep, happy that he had made a difference. Maybe this would give Jenny and Eduard a small chance. One hour later he woke up again with a tremendous thirst. He drank about a quarter gallon of water and threw up again afterwards. The dizziness was worse than before. August tottered out of his quarters and fell.

He was brought to the hospital ward. Most of the time he was passed out or dazed and confused, but he also had lucid moments. One time he heard somebody talking who sounded like the Warden.

"I can't have a dead president in my prison. This is the end. Why the hell did he have to come to my prison and why alone? I mean, who's that crazy to drive through that contamination?"

"It's radiation sickness. He won't last long. One, maybe two days. Hopefully by then the systems will be back up again and you can have him flown out. That way he will die somewhere else and we can tell everybody we rescued him."

"It's almost as if he wanted to come and see his daughter being executed. He might deserve that, but I don't."

Another time August heard people whispering.

"He had fifteen executed."

"He's a Nazi and he thinks this is his concentration camp."

"Forty-five inmates killed and over 200 suffocated because they knew what would happen if they gave up, and then he executes fifteen inmates for fifteen killed soldiers?!"

"He's a Nazi."

And then—a little more blurry—he heard a familiar female voice whispering. *Jenny.*

"Dad, they think I'm somebody else. Eduard too. Some protesters who tried to infiltrate the restricted area around Phoenix. They told us that they'll let us go if we leave the country and never return. I'm so sorry about what happened. Where is Mom? I love you, Dad. I have to go. They're coming."

<<<<To be continued>>>>

Thank you for purchasing my book. I hope you have enjoyed the story. If so (or even if not), please leave an honest review where you bought the eBook.

Reviews and social proof are the new currency that help independent authors get established and sell more books.

Appetite for more stories? Stories out and novels around the corner:

Manhunt

Book two of the *Peak Democracy* series

Three rebels have the power to restore civilization or dive deeper into total chaos...

Niklas is coming to terms with the destruction he's wrought. His data scramble crippled technology toppled the government and left the Eastern Seaboard a nuclear wasteland. He craves peace, but that's the last thing on the mind of those still in power...

Jenny is determined to not let her father's sacrifice be in vain. She and Eduard hold the code that could rewire humanity, but keeping that power from the new regime and their warlords could prove impossible...

In a land overrun by chaos, Niklas, Jenny, and Eduard must navigate a warped new world they created. And somehow, they must discover a place where they can rebuild their lives from the ashes...

Manhunt is the second book in the Peak Democracy series, a saga of near-future dystopian novels. If you like fully-imagined future worlds, dynamic characters, and high-stakes adventure, then you'll love G.D. Leon's exhilarating sequel.

Release date is set for October 31st. Sign up to my mailing list at http://www.gd-leon.com/readers-group-pd for more updates and to know when it's ready for pre-order.

Unleashed
Book three of the *Peak Democracy* series

Torn between revenge and survival, one man has the power to save civilization...

Niklas has left the divided United States far behind. In the aftermath of the data purge that brought the world to its knees, he's found peace running a Patagonian hostel with the woman of his dreams. It's almost enough to make him forget he's a wanted man...

When rising powers begin revamping the fragile data system, Niklas learns the powers-that-be haven't forgotten his role in the data catastrophe. And they'll hunt down everyone Niklas loves to make him pay...

Niklas must team up with the growing rebellion to unleash a cyber weapon only he can yield. To safeguard the peace he left behind, Niklas must plunge headlong into war...

Unleashed is the final novel in the Peak Democracy series, a trilogy of chillingly-real dystopian tales. If you like fully-imagined future realities, complex characters, and rebellions against all odds, then you'll love the thrilling conclusion to G.D. Leon's thought-provoking series.

Release date is set for February 2018. Intrigued? Sign up to my mailing list at http://www.gd-leon.com/readers-group-pd for more updates and to know when it's ready for pre-order.

The Frigorifico
Literary Fiction, published August 2016

A dying town. A family on the rocks. Can Ruben break the cycle of destruction before he loses it all?

Ruben and the entire town of Santa Rita, Argentina depend on the Frigorifico, a major factory and the town's main source of work. When the factory closes down, Ruben must make a choice: hope for a reopening or start over somewhere else. After deciding to move, Ruben must do so without any of his family or loved ones. As he makes a new life for himself in Buenos Aires, he watches the situation in Santa Rita deteriorate.

The most disturbing part is that his brother, Frede, is immersed in the violence that continues to spread. And as a result, everyone Ruben loves has drifted into harm's way. When tragedy strikes, despite his best efforts, Ruben must come to terms with the past, the present, and what will become of the future.

The Frigorifico is a work of literary fiction for the 99%. If you like powerful storytelling, real characters, and literature that peels back the curtain of today's society, then you'll love G.D. Leon's chilling look back into a bygone era.

This book can be found on Amazon, Apple iBooks and Kobo.

AUTHOR'S NOTE

While developing the idea for this story, I realized I must have a vision of the future, not only the part I describe, but a comprehensive view on where the world will be in 25 years.

The research and development of ideas were some of the hardest but also the funniest parts of writing the trilogy, and I don't want to withhold that. Please find the visual inspirations on Pinterest (http://www.pinterest.com/gd_leon)

Energy

A terrorist attack on Palos Verde led to a rethinking with nuclear power plants, similar to the Fukushima effect. Two technologies benefit by getting their long-expected boost in the plateau of productivity: Solar power and batteries.

Solar power develops so far that modern houses and half of all US cities are self-sustainable. Even textiles, such as heavy canvas, can contain solar power cells, a feature extremely successful with sailboats. And enormous batteries help cities to get through the night and winter. Batteries also helped electronic cars to arrive on main street. Fueled cars remain only relevant for special purposes, such as large and heavy trucks, planes, race cars, and nostalgic people; however, gas stations became rare.

The impact on the oil industry is significant: All major companies went under or transformed into renewable energy or specialty chemical companies. In addition, the slump of demand for oil leads to an economic crisis in Arabic countries and to a Pan-Arabic civil war that lasts 10 years and reshapes the surface of the entire region.

Biofuel was predicted to be on the rise for two years; however, it was overhauled by solar power/batteries

Food

The meat industry went through the same as the Tobacco industry. Large lawsuits and pressure from the public lead to two developments:

- Real meat production is downsized and meat becomes enormously expensive. This leads to a vicious downward circle: less demand, less revenues, meat prices fell for a short time until more and more farms switched to crops. This led to inefficiencies in distribution and to overly high prices.
- Second, cultivated meat becomes more popular. At first, meat replacements boom, but then artificial meat farms pop up in the industrial belt of major cities, growing meat based on food engineering.

Gimmicks: Meat is tagged so you could get back to the animal it is from (including the entire food chain). Of the remaining people that could afford meat, most people wouldn't look at the details, as they don't want to know too much; they are fine with getting a green flag. With vegetables; however, the feature was a best-seller. People were able to trace their vegetables and fruits back to the farm and the location in the field, including when it was fertilized and harvested and which pesticides were used.

Global Warming

Large weather patterns did not change; however, they intensified.

More extreme storms and, with them, more flooding occurred.

In general, warmer weather and extended heat periods led to more bugs/mosquitos and more tropical diseases further north (Malaria/Dengue etc.).

Cities/towns try to protect from flooding by mandating newly built constructions and major rebuilding to add absorbing wells. And they require plant watering, car washing, and even swimming pools to be filled out of the well (not from fresh water). Water shortages support a new industry: desalination (see other technologies below).

Climate changes US

- Northeast: Hot and crowded with higher tidal surges, leading to large infrastructure investment needs.
- Southeast: Higher frequency of category 4 and 5 hurricanes. Also, higher tidal surges impact Florida and Louisiana, especially.
- Midwest: Warming lakes leading to overall increase of algae and dying fish population (aquatic acidification).
- Great plains: Increased drought severity and heat waves in the south, warmer winters and increased precipitation

in the northern part. Kansas City is the first major city running out of water.

- Southwest: Hotter and dryer, hitting agriculture hard (less water, more bugs).
- Northwest: Increased rain (lest snow), affecting hydropower in summer. Therefore, hydropower is not an option after the attack on the nuclear power plant in Palos Verde.

Large scale project to store CO_2 in the Rockies to reduce CO_2 in the atmosphere was planned, but was delayed due to ongoing discussions whether global warming was man-made.

Diseases/Health care

Results of cancer therapy have been improved, mainly because of improved cancer markers and early therapies: Cancer checks every three months are normal, and there are even some simple home cancer checks. However, they are not appreciated, as they still give too many false positives.

There was one pandemic flu in 2022, killing mostly elderly people, as all known anti-biotics failed. This freed up billions of funds in pension systems. Hedge funds approached the pensions, offering them lucrative investments with the effect that conglomerates, like the holding, became possible (see also Economy).

Research has found a penicillin replacement. However, the replacement is less effective than antibiotics. Standard treatment remains antibiotics, and only resistant cases are treated with the new remedy, giving patients at least a 50% increased chance to survive.

While they found vaccines and remedies against major diseases (HIV, Ebola etc.), some diseases came back due to negligence and misinformation: Measles (vaccine ignorance), cholera (water problems and flooding, mainly in Southern Cities), and tuberculosis (resistant strains, leading to checks at immigration and quarantine of infected people).

Hospitals have sealed boxes for every patient that comes in sick, and until they know what it is and if they can treat it, the patient remains in this box.

Highest-risk populations cannot access new treatments for chronic disease. 48% of US residents live with one or more chronic conditions. Behavioral deficiencies of people lead to the increase of chronic conditions, and governmental programs, focusing on nudging people, fail as people adapt too quickly. Insurance will lower premiums if you agree to use your AI PA to nudge you.

Social life

Dating: In the cities, the single with changing relations and patchwork families is a normal state (There are apps connecting people based on interests and closeness. Some go even as far as including genetic compatibility. In rural areas, however, despite cell phone coverage and apps supporting automated matching, dating is still traditional, mainly driven by the limited population.

Social networks: Sharing live views (people watch it on google glasses/contact lenses).

Being offline as a hype peaked in 2025 and is on the descent. However, only 85% of the population is constantly online. 2% are voluntarily offline, and 13% are pushed out of the system and can't afford to be online.

Immigration causes higher friction than ever for various reasons: labor, diseases (people are health screened at immigration). People with visas are tagged and followed/locatable. The task to locate illegal immigrants with overrun visas is outsourced to private companies, such as The Holding. They use the tagging mechanism and social media. Both basic civil rights (tagging/being locatable and access to social media) is given up when applying for a visa.

Former minorities make up 50% of the US population (24% Hispanic, 14% Asian, 13% African American). Spanish and Chinese had become quasi-official languages.

Housing

Gentrification of former affordable zones lead to a push out of lower middle class to far away suburbs (large co-op cities).

Housing in the center becomes almost unaffordable, leading to empty city centers. Town centers outside downtown or in the suburbs become more important, leading to a decentralization again.

Cities develop differently: Key cities continue to be their own micro-cosmos (New York, Los Angeles, Boston, Washington D.C., Miami, San Francisco, Houston etc.). Mid-sized cities are on ups and downs like waves. As of 2030, for example, Burlington, VT was on the way up, Fairview, MT was created artificially, while Charleston is on the decline due to increased flooding.

In cities close to the ocean, ground level stores became cheaper due to repeated flooding. And buildings in the center connected on the first floor, similar to downtown Calgary.

Modern apartments in major cities don't have fully fledged kitchens anymore to save space. Delivery will become the common way to eat.

Economy

The largest issue for the economy will be that a large portion of people will not be employed anymore, especially in the services. A combination of automation/AI/machine learning (see below) will push them out of employment.

On the back of the lack of jobs, they will take on a broad variety of app-based self-employment opportunities (extension of earlier offerings, such as UBER, Airbnb if they have capital, KDP, Fiverr etc.).

Additionally, due to the higher life expectancy and the missing 401k savings, many must work until their mid-seventies.

Developed sharing economy: Vacation rental, IT space (Virtual Machine is common and software is not owned, but rented). However, outside of limousine services, cars remain mainly owned, especially outside major cities.

People got scared by ongoing economic instability and volatility. They bought physical gold as security, creating a new business:

renting out old army bunkers (and partial spaces) to have the gold stored safely.

Moves in industries (food/sharing/data/AI replacement) lead to less industrial/agriculture and low-skilled service jobs. Shortage of traditional jobs lead to further frictions.

Real-time translation for all major languages, allowing speech-to-speech translation; however, some difficulties with dialects remain.

Nano/quantum technology

Technology made impressive progress, allowing several crucial developments:

- Solar panels in textiles
- Shrinking batteries to allow for larger amount of power stored in smaller/lighter batteries
- Nano 3D-printers
- Quantum computers

Space travel

Two civil (hotels) and four military space stations (surveillance and warfare (only US) were built with weekly taxi service. Shuttles are not launched like space shuttles anymore, but more like planes leaving the earth's atmosphere.

Moon base was planned by NASA for years, but not realized, as there was no benefit. The Holding is the first one trying this endeavor.

Mars mission is planned, and the space ship is being built outside the US space station.

Bio-mechanics/implants

Body implants are advanced, except for the brain. Entire eyes and ears can be replaced; however, the replacement is less effective than the natural ear/eye due to interface problems with the nerves. For the same reason, brain implants are not advanced either (several military research projects are running). 3D printing allows for efficient in-surgery printing of prosthesis.

Thought reading systems are in early test phase with military research projects.

Eugenie advanced until 2025 into a space where people could select certain genomes to be added/changed in a very expensive process. The results were devastating (similar to Contergan): Mental illnesses, prone to certain specific diseases (standard ones with deadly impact) and increased number of dysplasia.

Other technologies

WiFi: Complete coverage (even in the Rockies) due to improved satellite connections and ground antennas.

Water desalination progressed. Carry-on desalination systems are common on boats and in households close to the sea. The desalination membranes were also found to clean water—therefore, in recent years, the systems got increasingly popular in areas not close to the ocean, although certain industrial toxic waste can't be filtered out by the membrane.

Hypersonic flight: There is a large arsenal in cruise missiles and two special military planes. Civil aircrafts are still in test phase, and the biggest problem has turned out that passengers are getting sick (there were even some casualties).

Unlimited data storage and access in the cloud.

Trillions of sensors, including implantable sensors for body heat etc. Clothing with embedded chips (pick up data from body sensors for adjustments to clothing, emergency GPS, starting car/opening door body sensors get to 99% accuracy of who is wearing the clothes for robbery protection).

3D printing will allow printing the material for entire cars or houses. Also, 3D printing will be used in hospitals for printing supplies or implants.

Gimmicks:

- Contact lenses like google glasses. They change color with the mood, based on the blood vessels in your eye.

- Smartphones, or what's left of them, will connect to the VM in the office to activate licensed Software and access office features. From a look and feel perspective, they are nothing more than a shell to allow connectivity and iden-tification: no speaker or microphone, minimal display as content is projected on nearby interactive surfaces (win-dows, mirrors, glasses etc.).

AI/Robotics

Driverless cars will only be allowed with a driver, still holding the steering wheel (like an improved autopilot). Several accidents with lawsuits against car companies and supplying IT companies led to verdicts and laws bringing the driver back into the responsibility (i.e., the only way a driver can claim the company is guilty is if he can prove he held the steering wheel). Agriculture machines will be 70% driverless; however, the machines are only rented, not owned by the farms (service vs owning).

AI personal assistants will be omnipresent. They will know everything about us (behaviors, tendencies, preferences, and usual responses). Depending on the level of freedom given by their owner, AI personal assistants will be able to answer e-mails, book appointments, or act on behalf of their owners in social media with the funny consequence that AIs will talk to AIs. AIs will be programmed to anticipate their owner's needs, such as going for a drink Friday night (e.g., they will ask the AI of a buddy, and funny enough, they both will appear).

AI will make large parts of lawyer services obsolete (filling in forms, filing status for immigration, fighting parking tickets, etc.). Taxes will be filled in by AI personal assistants (as they know all financial details anyway), and one can avoid being audited by the IRS by simply allowing the IRS to access your AI PA finance part. AI takes over tasks in Finance/Banking (interpreting commercial-loan agreements, request insurance policy updates from home-owners etc.).

AIs will replace 50% of service jobs (call center, banking/finance, pharmacists, etc.).

ACKNOWLEDGEMENTS

Thanks to everybody who made this book possible.

The feedback and input of my beta readers, Marius Holzer, Richa Singh, Camille Studer, Melissa (littlemissproof@ Fiverr), and Michaela Breuss, were crucial to make the story rock solid.

Additional thanks go to the professionals helping me to polish my words and create the beautiful look and feel: Clare Diston (edit and proofread), Simon Avery (cover design), Bryan Cohen (sales description).

I also don't want to miss the chance (again) to thank all the people who help other authors by showing the way, including all trial and error: Joanna Penn with her Creative Penn podcast, Jim Kuckral and Bryan Cohen with their Sell More Books Show, and Joel Friedlander, who taught me to cherish the inside of the book as much as the outside.

Last but not least, I want to thank my wife for her invaluable support that allowed me to write this book.

ABOUT G.D. LEON
================

G.D. Leon is a novelist with roots in the German language.

Gilbert David Leon's journey brought him from Zurich, where he grew up, to the greater New York area, where he lives with his beautiful wife. Stations on his journey included Berlin and Buenos Aires, leaving impressions that remain until today. Even though it has been more than a decade since he left Buenos Aires, he still enjoys drinking mate, playing Truco and listening to Argentinian music, from tango to folk music.

He has a bachelor's in Business Administration from the University of Applied Science, Zurich, a master's degree in MIS/IT from the University of Wales, and a master's in Business Administration from the Robert H. Smith School of Business at the University of Maryland, College Park.

Outside writing, sports and reading have been given spots on Gilbert's agenda, and he loves to travel the US and the world. Other hobbies include old books and book sales. He can spend hours hunting treasures, and usually he ends up with one or two boxes of used books.

Connect with Gilbert online:

(e) gd(at)gd-leon.com

(w) www.gd-leon.com

(f) http://www.facebook.com/gilbertdavidleon

(p) www.pinterest.com/gd_leon

49043630R00150

Made in the USA
Middletown, DE
04 October 2017